Little Mouse
Gets Ready

A TOON BOOK BY
JEFF SMITH

TOON BOOKS IS AN IMPRINT OF CANDLEWICK PRESS

A THEODOR SEUSS GEISEL HONOR BOOK
A SCHOOL LIBRARY JOURNAL BEST COMICS FOR KIDS
A JUNIOR LIBRARY GUILD SELECTION

For Kathleen Glosan

Editorial Director: FRANÇOISE MOULY

Book Design: JONATHAN BENNETT & FRANÇOISE MOULY

Colors: STEVE HAMAKER

JEFF SMITH'S artwork was drawn in black ink on paper and digitally colored.

A TOON Book™ © 2009 Jeff Smith & RAW Junior, LLC, 27 Greene Street, New York, NY 10013. TOON Books® is an imprint of Candlewick Press, 99 Dover Street, Somerville, MA 02144. No part of this book may be used or reproduced in any manner whatsoever without written permission except in the case of brief quotations embodied in critical articles and reviews. All rights reserved. TOON Books®, LITTLE LIT® and TOON Into Reading!™ are trademarks of RAW Junior, LLC. Printed in Dongguan, Guangdong, China by Toppan Leefung. The Library of Congress has cataloged the hardcover edition as follows:
Smith, Jeff, 1960 Feb. 27-   Little Mouse gets ready / by Jeff Smith.   p. cm.   "A TOON Book."   Summary: Little Mouse gets dressed to go to the barn with his mother, brothers, and sisters.   ISBN 978-1-935179-01-6 (hardcover) 1. Graphic novels. [1. Graphic novels. 2. Mice—Fiction. 3. Clothing and dress—Fiction.] I. Title.
PZ7.7.S64Li 2009   741.5'973–dc22   2008055403
ISBN 978-1-935179-24-5 (paperback)
13 14 15 16 17 18 TPN 10 9 8 7 6 5 4 3 2 1
WWW.TOON-BOOKS.COM

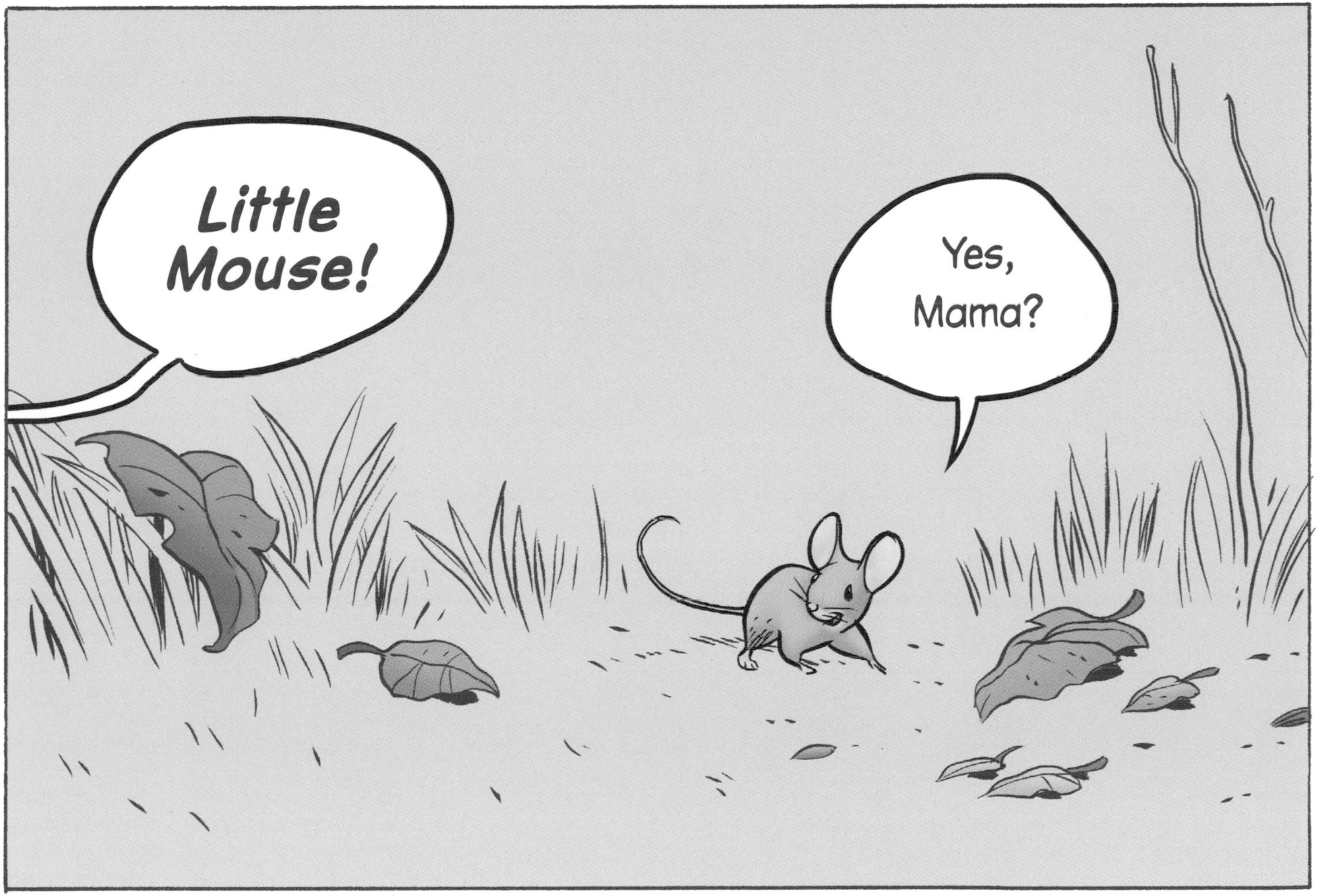
Little Mouse!
Yes, Mama?

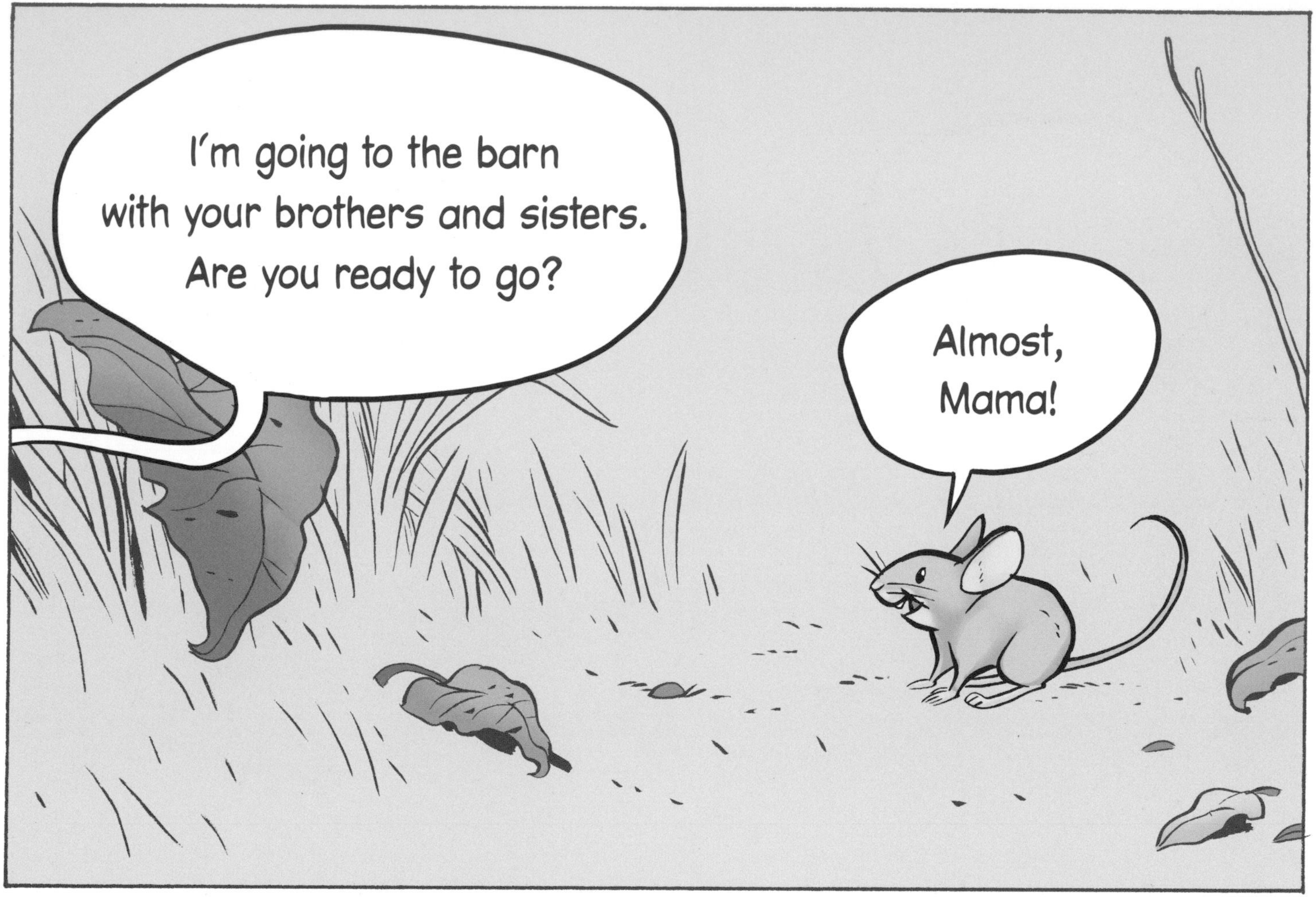
I'm going to the barn with your brothers and sisters. Are you ready to go?
Almost, Mama!

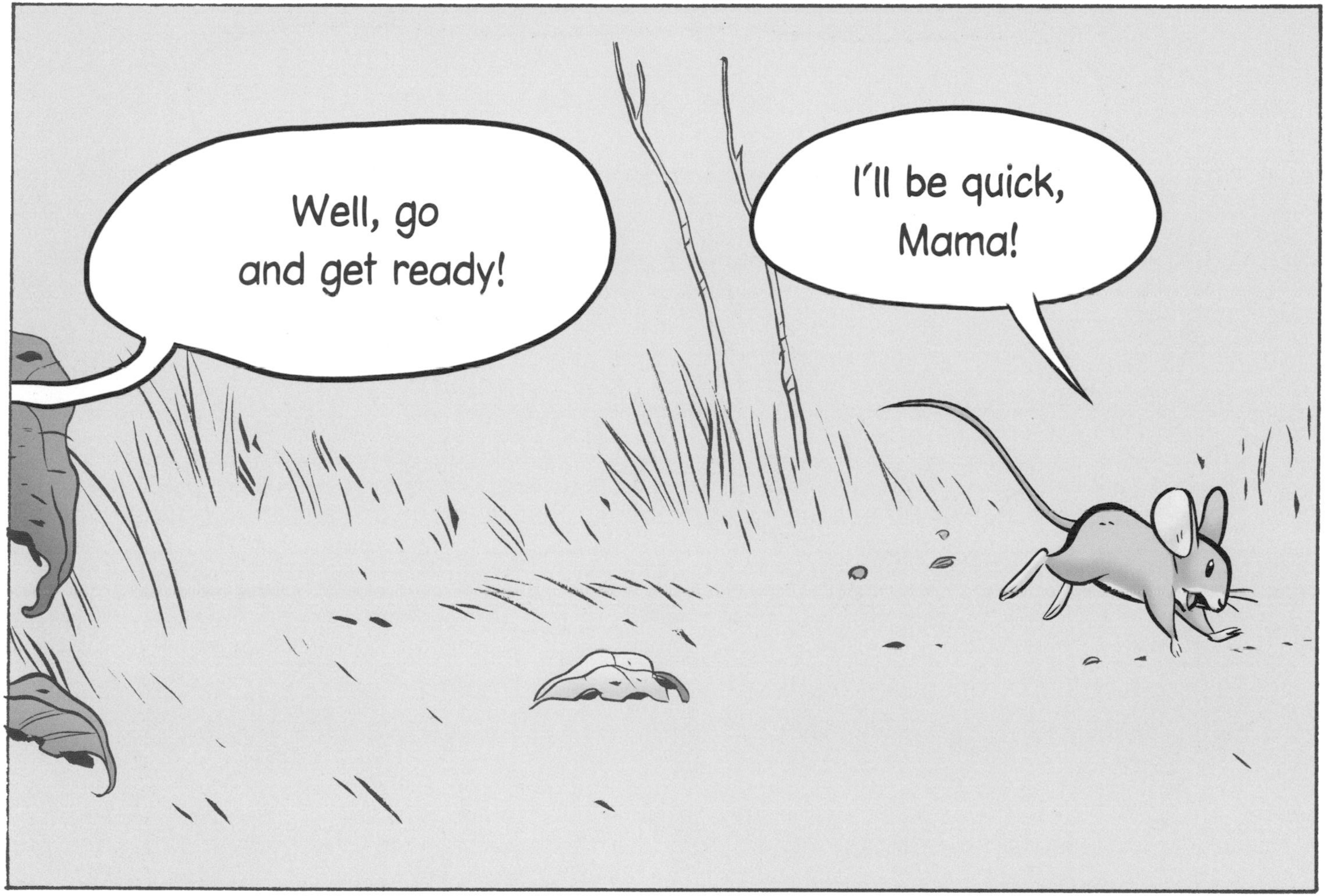
Well, go and get ready!
I'll be quick, Mama!

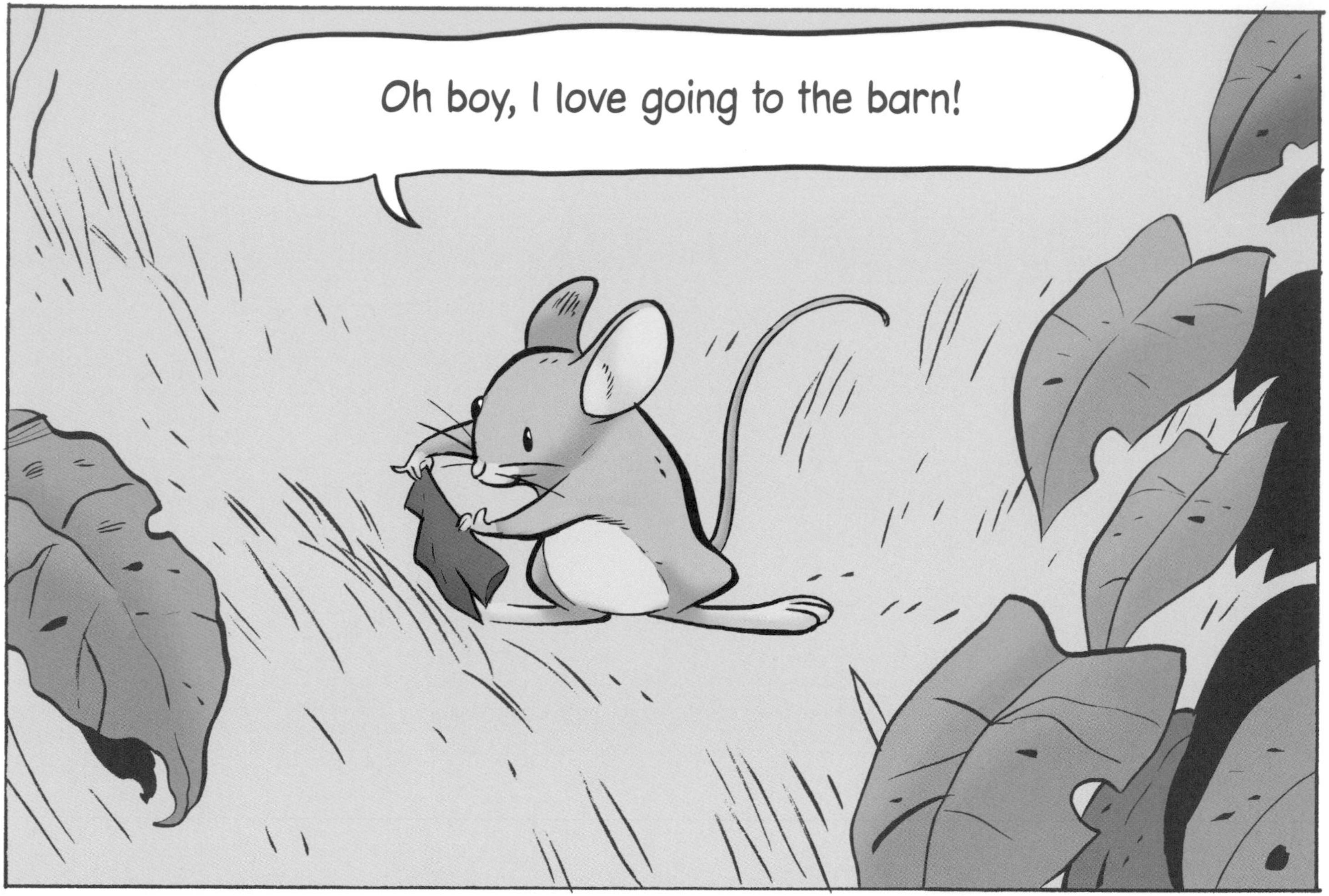
Oh boy, I love going to the barn!

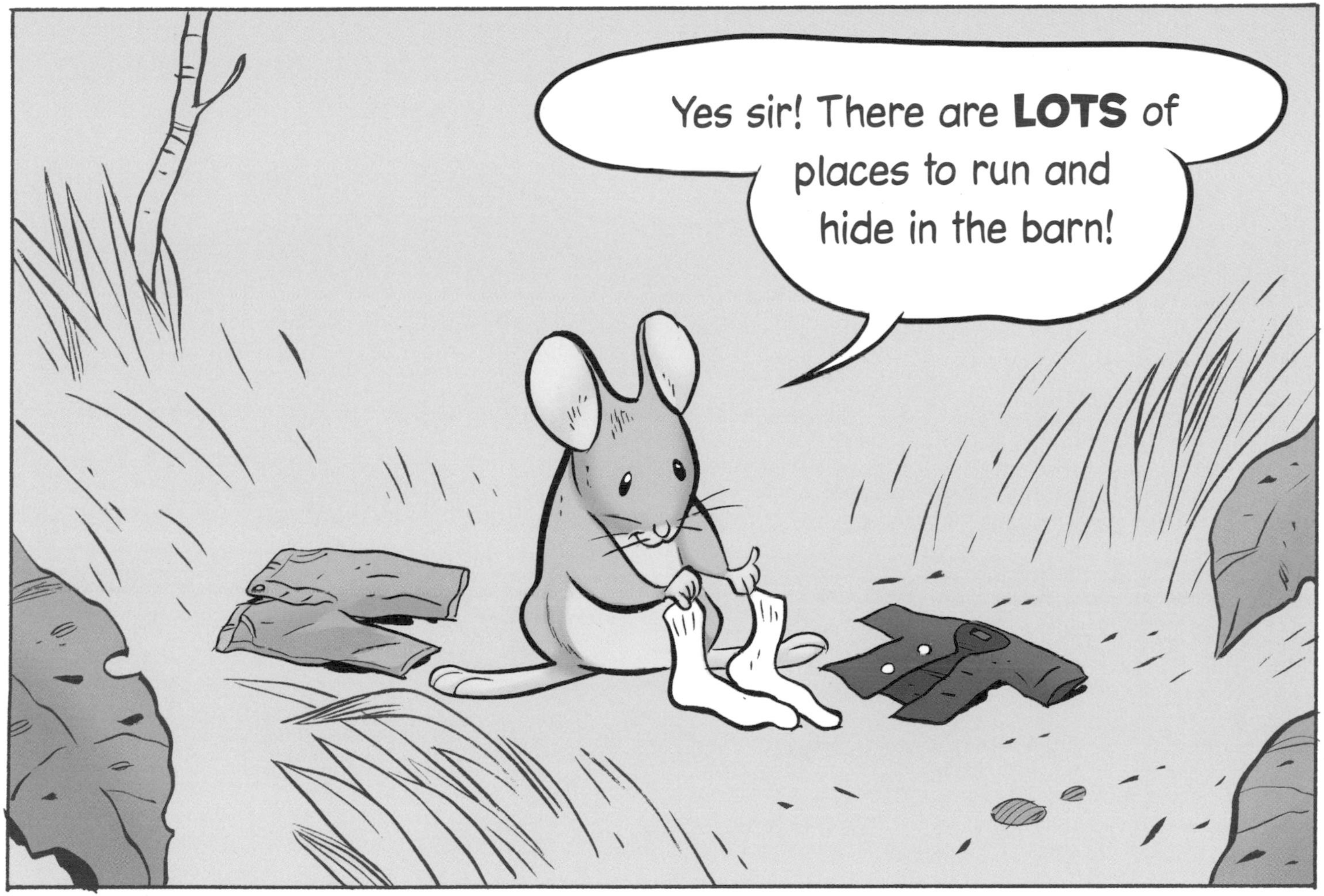
Yes sir! There are **LOTS** of places to run and hide in the barn!

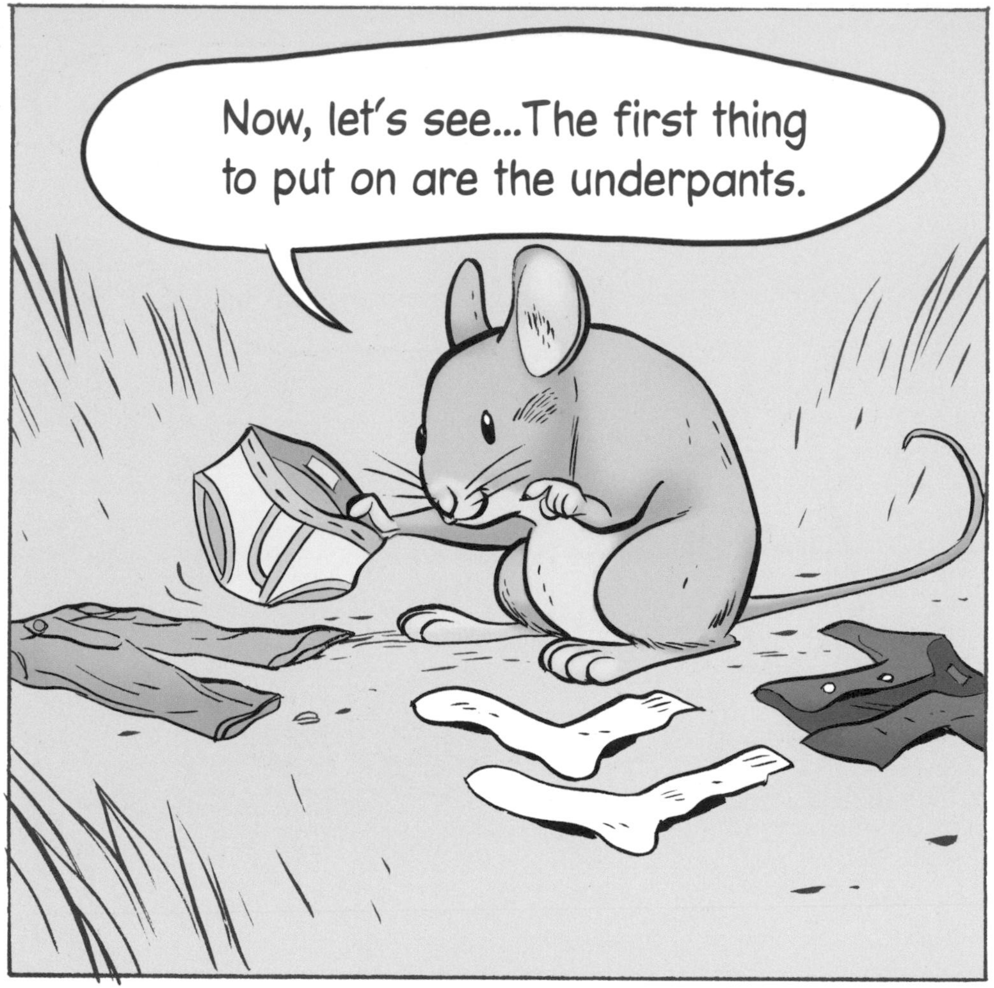
Now, let's see...The first thing to put on are the underpants.

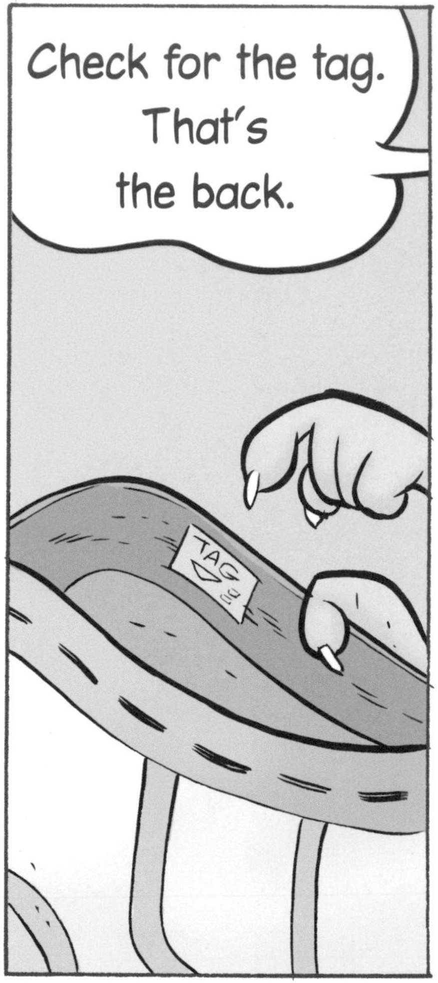
Check for the tag. That's the back.
TAG

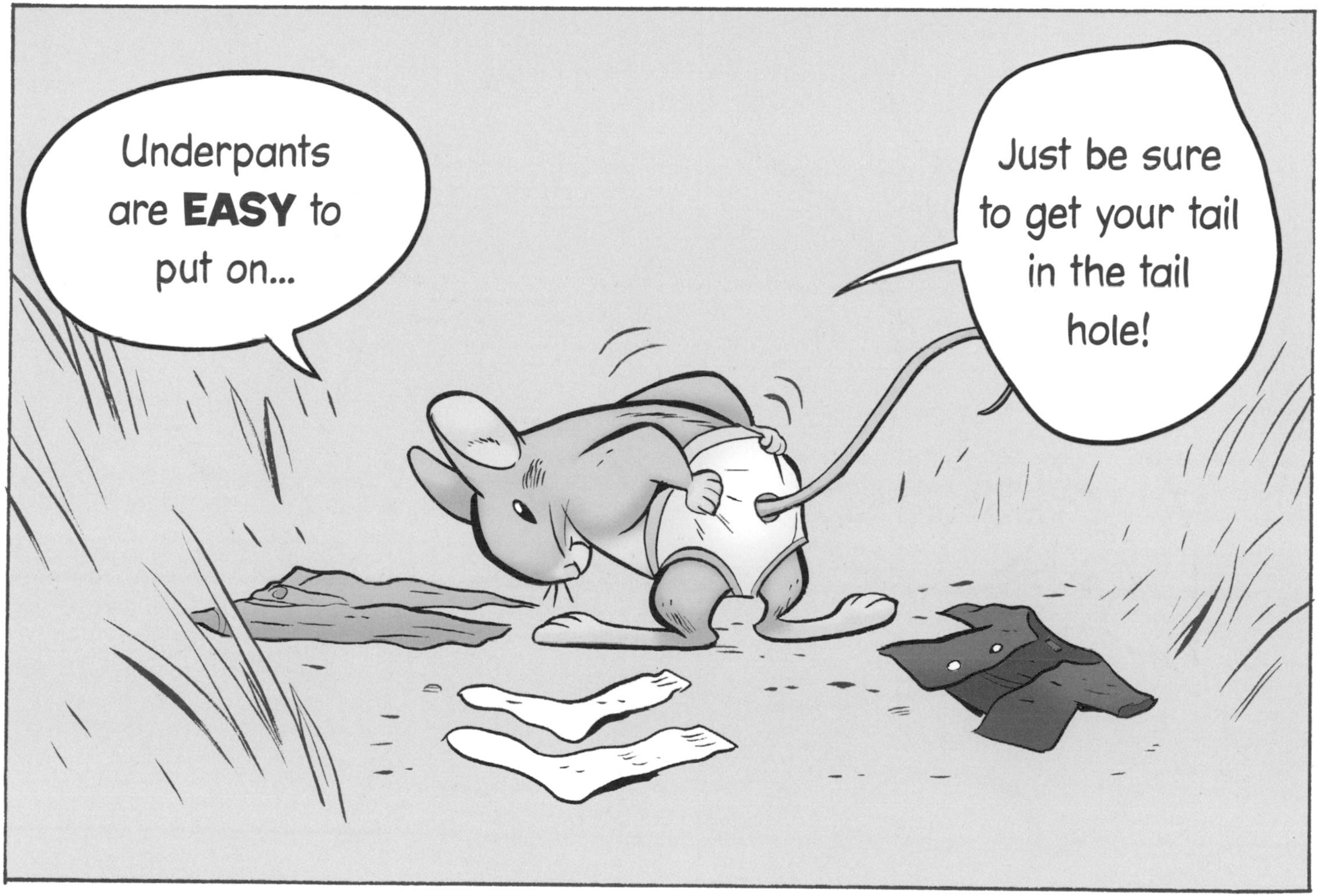
Underpants are **EASY** to put on...
Just be sure to get your tail in the tail hole!

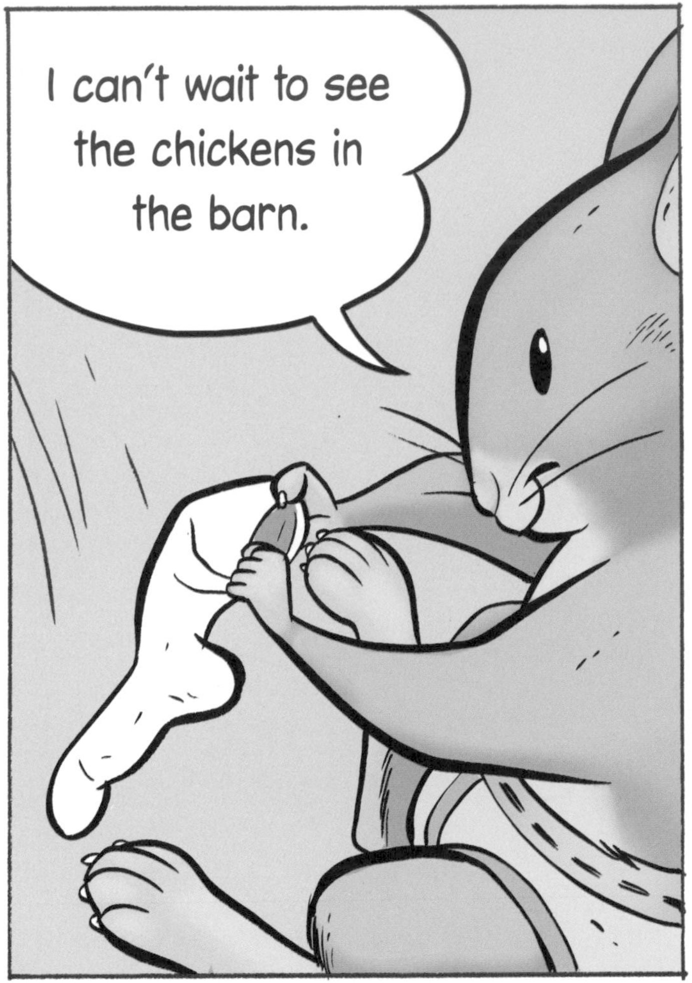
I can't wait to see the chickens in the barn.

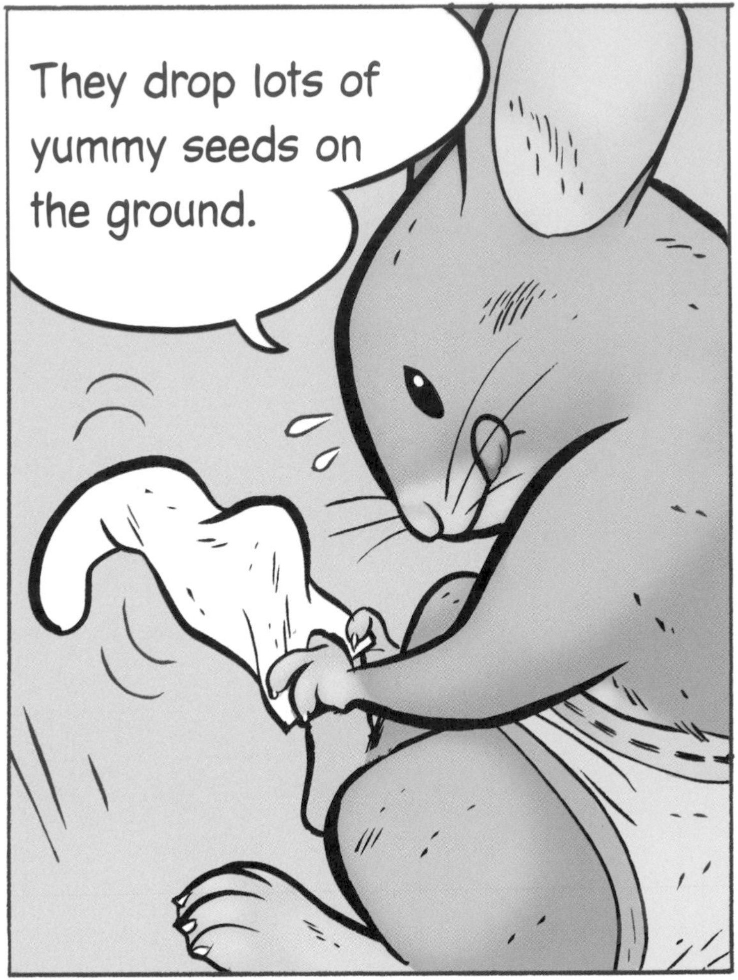
They drop lots of yummy seeds on the ground.

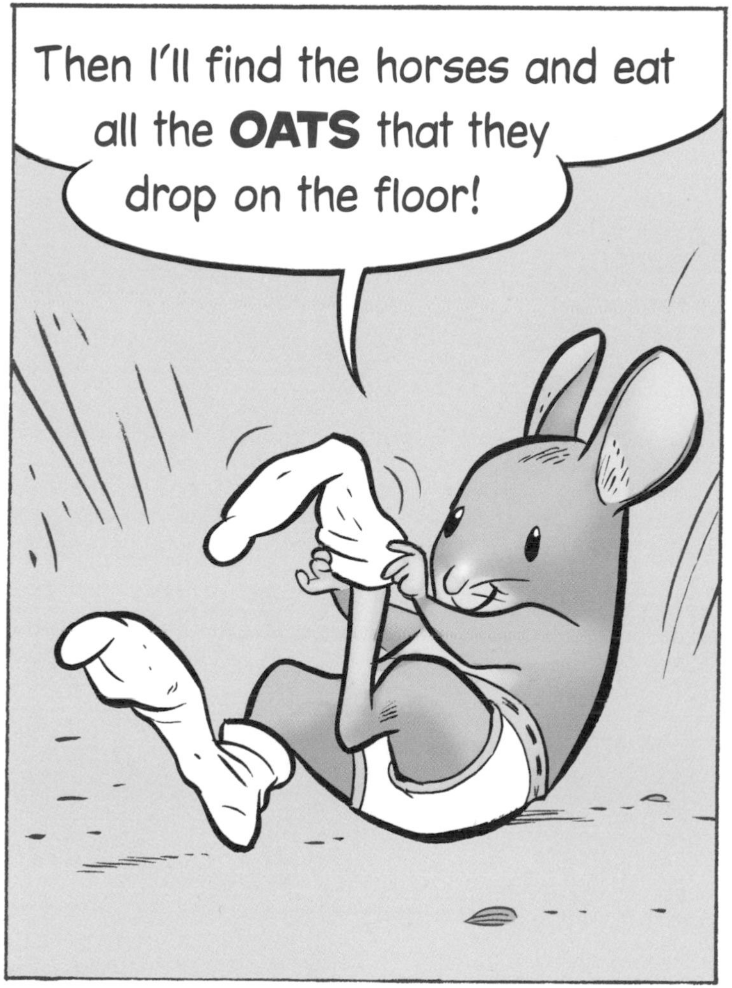
Then I'll find the horses and eat all the **OATS** that they drop on the floor!

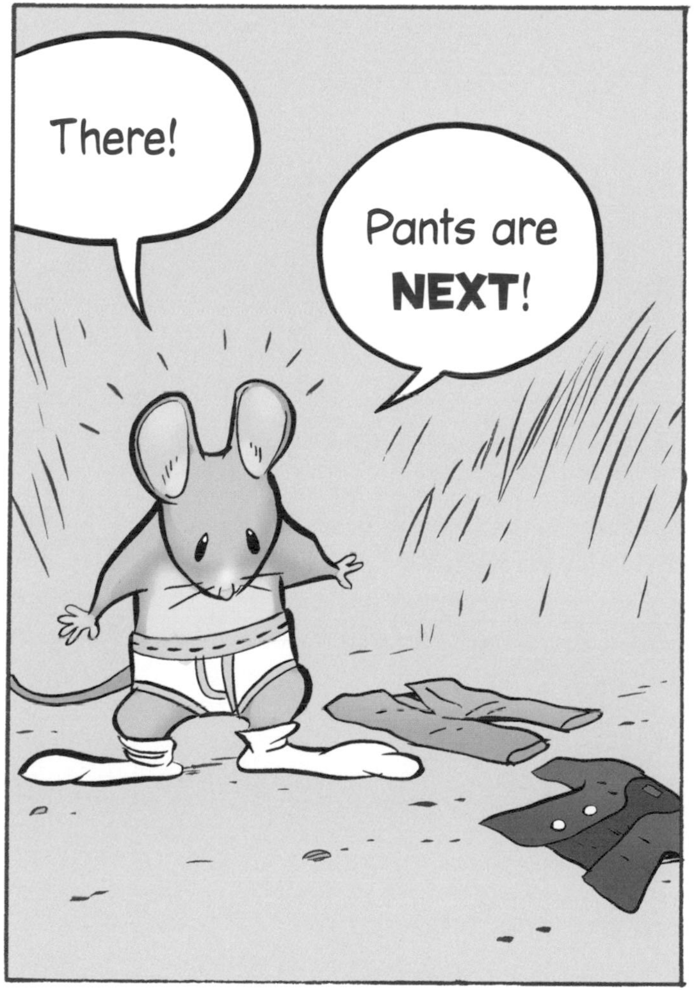
There!
Pants are **NEXT**!

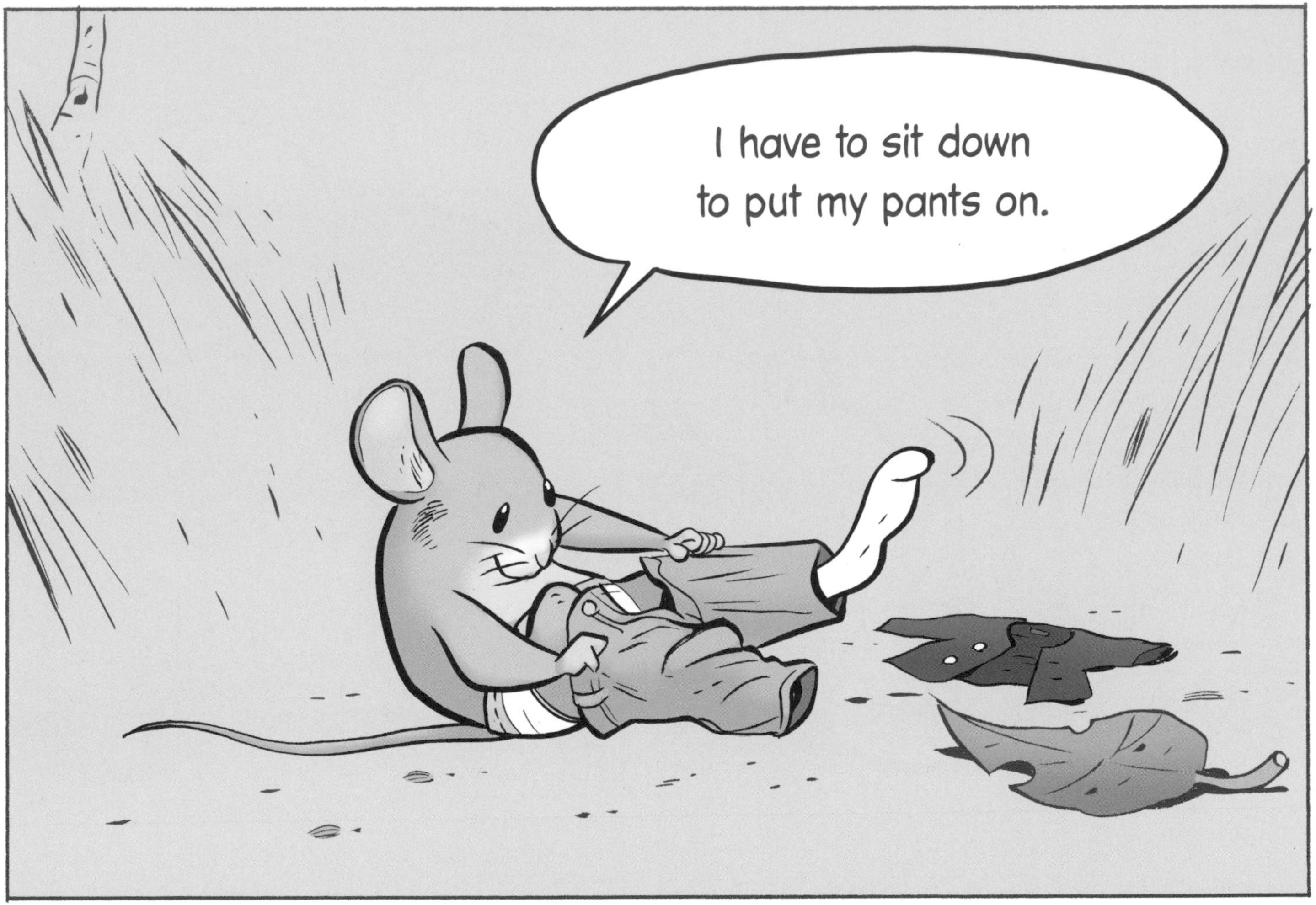
I have to sit down
to put my pants on.

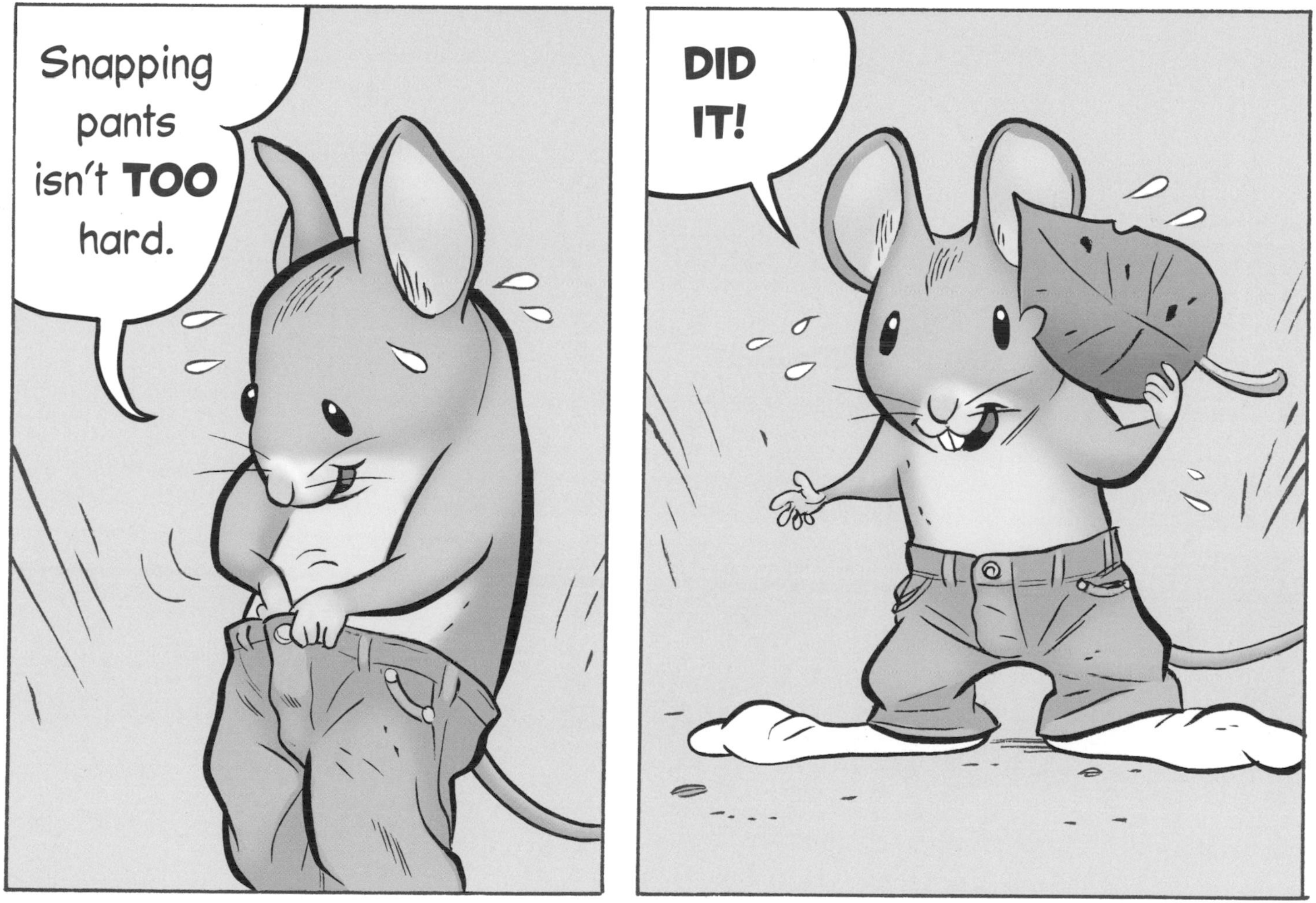
Snapping pants isn't **TOO** hard.
DID IT!

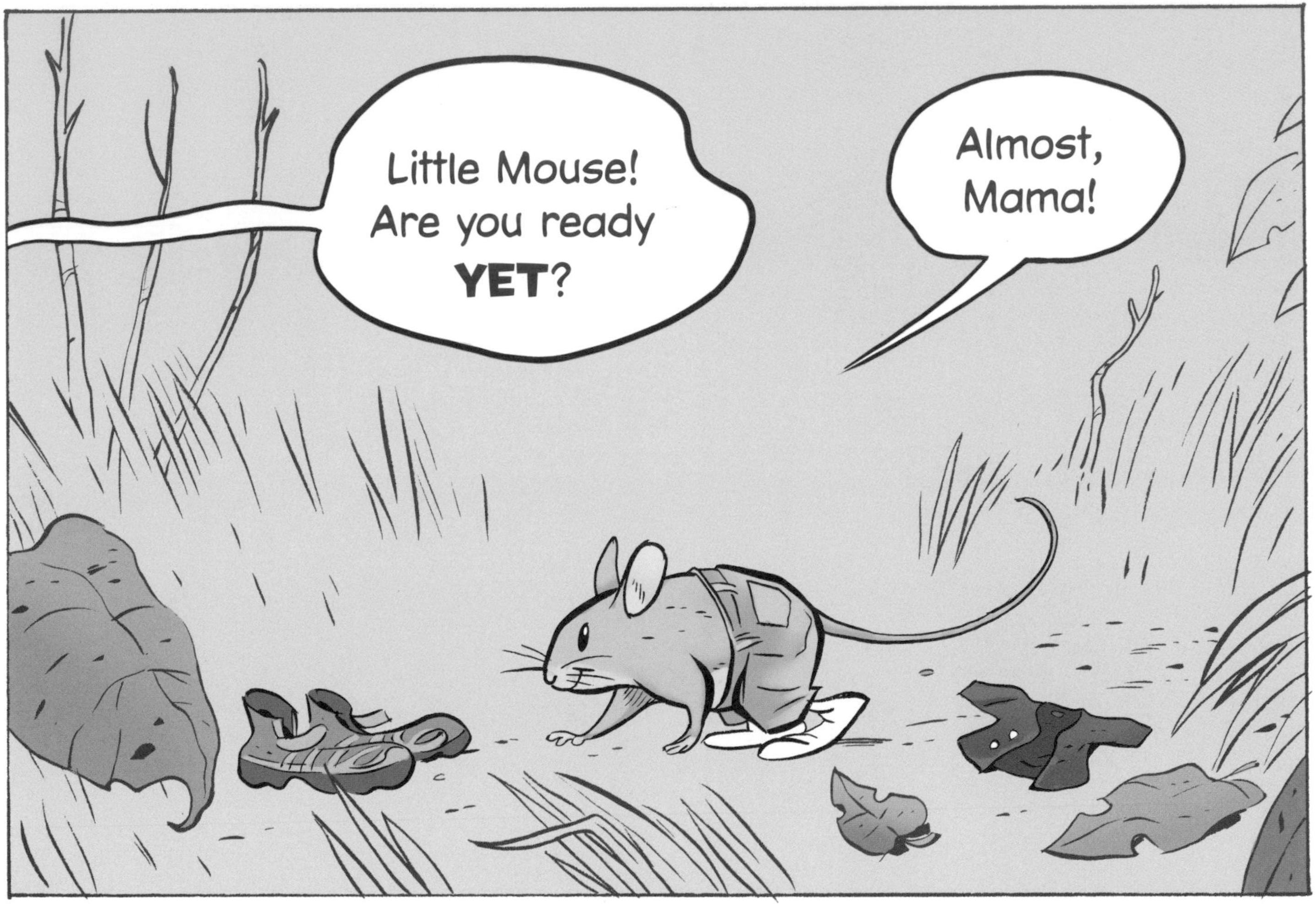
Little Mouse! Are you ready **YET**?
Almost, Mama!

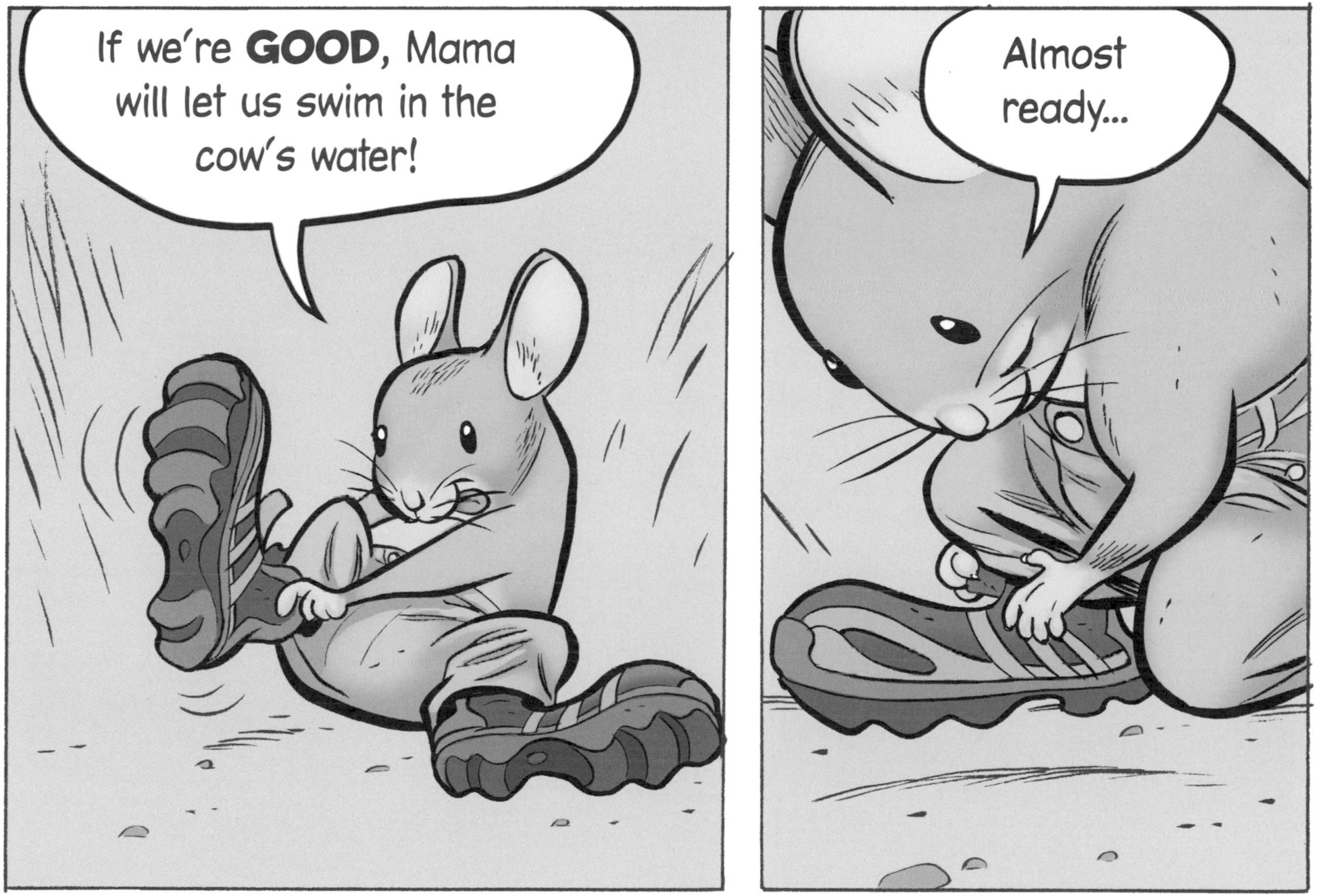
If we're **GOOD**, Mama will let us swim in the cow's water!
Almost ready...

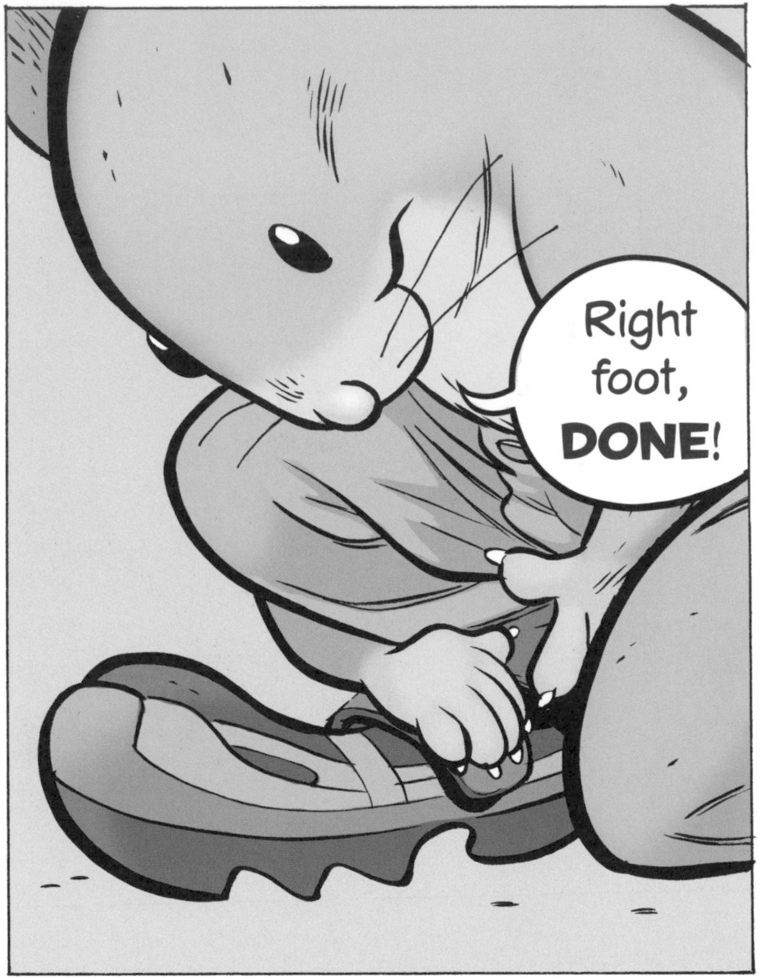
Right foot, **DONE**!

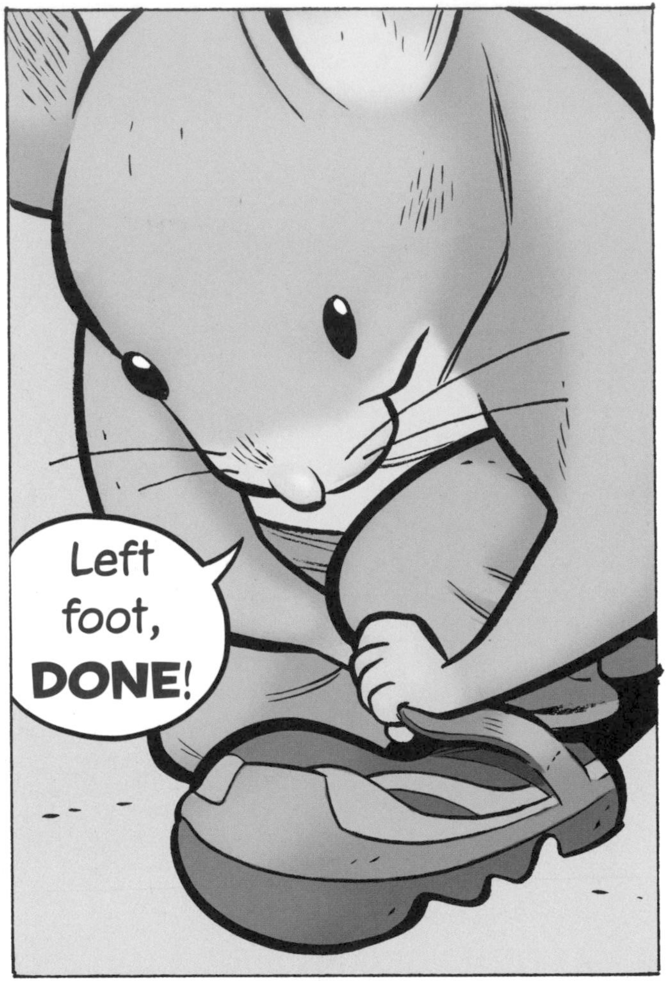
Left foot, **DONE**!

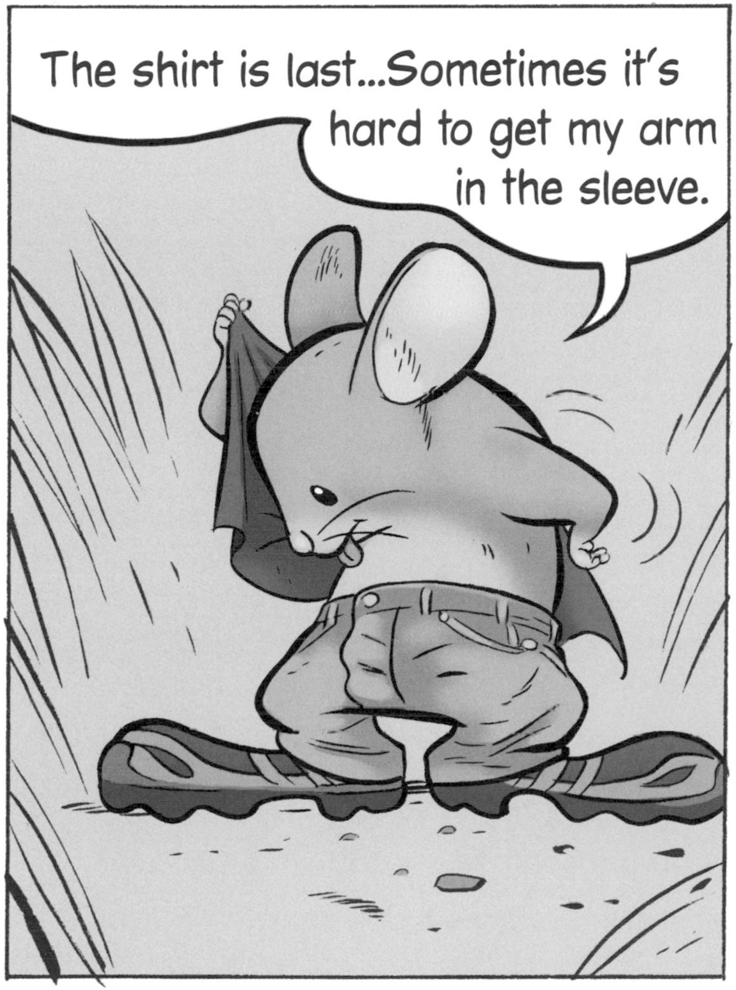
The shirt is last...Sometimes it's hard to get my arm in the sleeve.

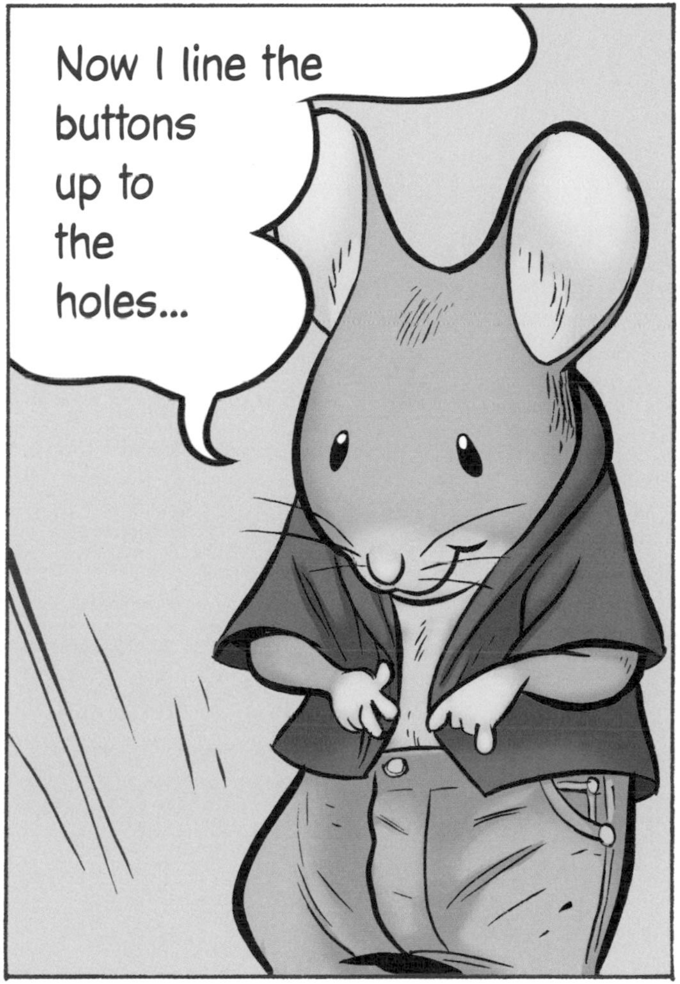
Now I line the buttons up to the holes...

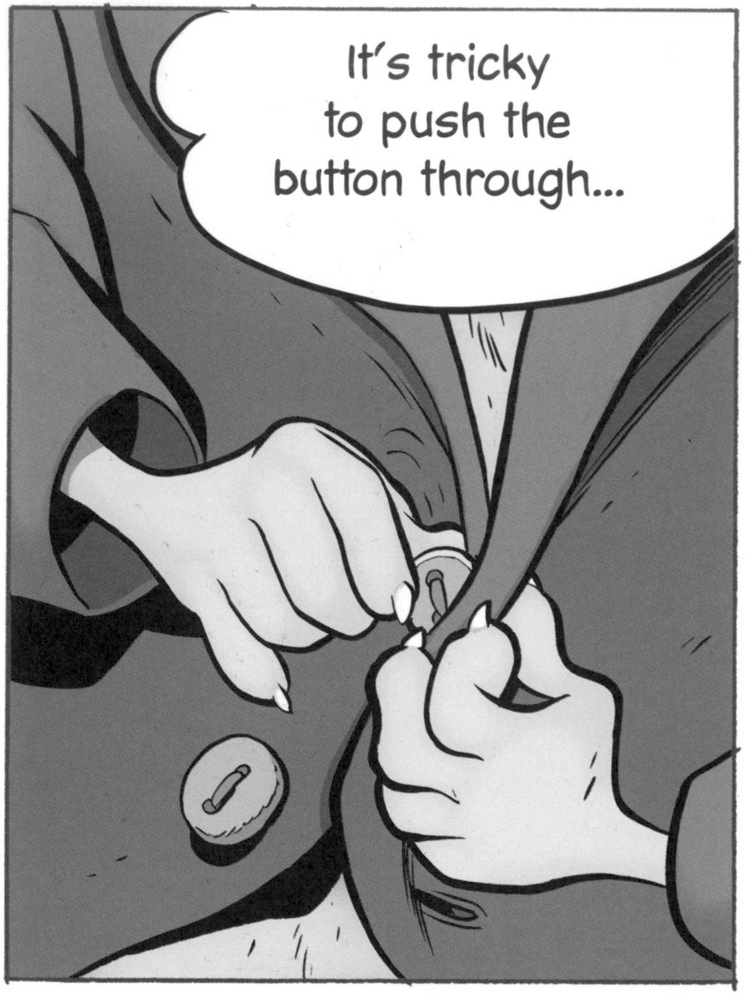
It's tricky to push the button through...

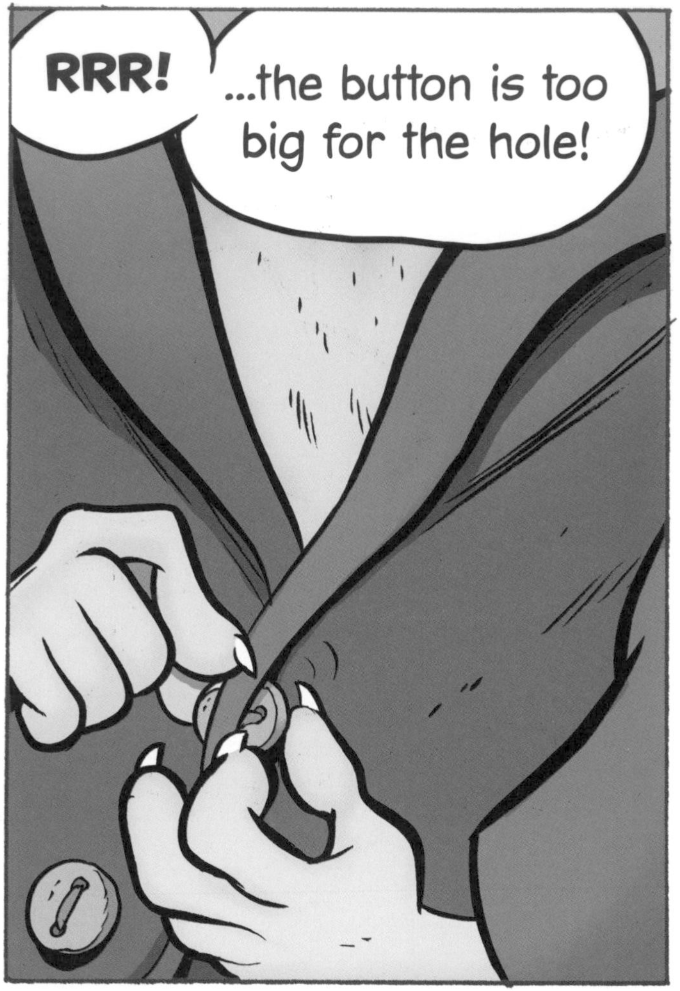
RRR!
...the button is too big for the hole!

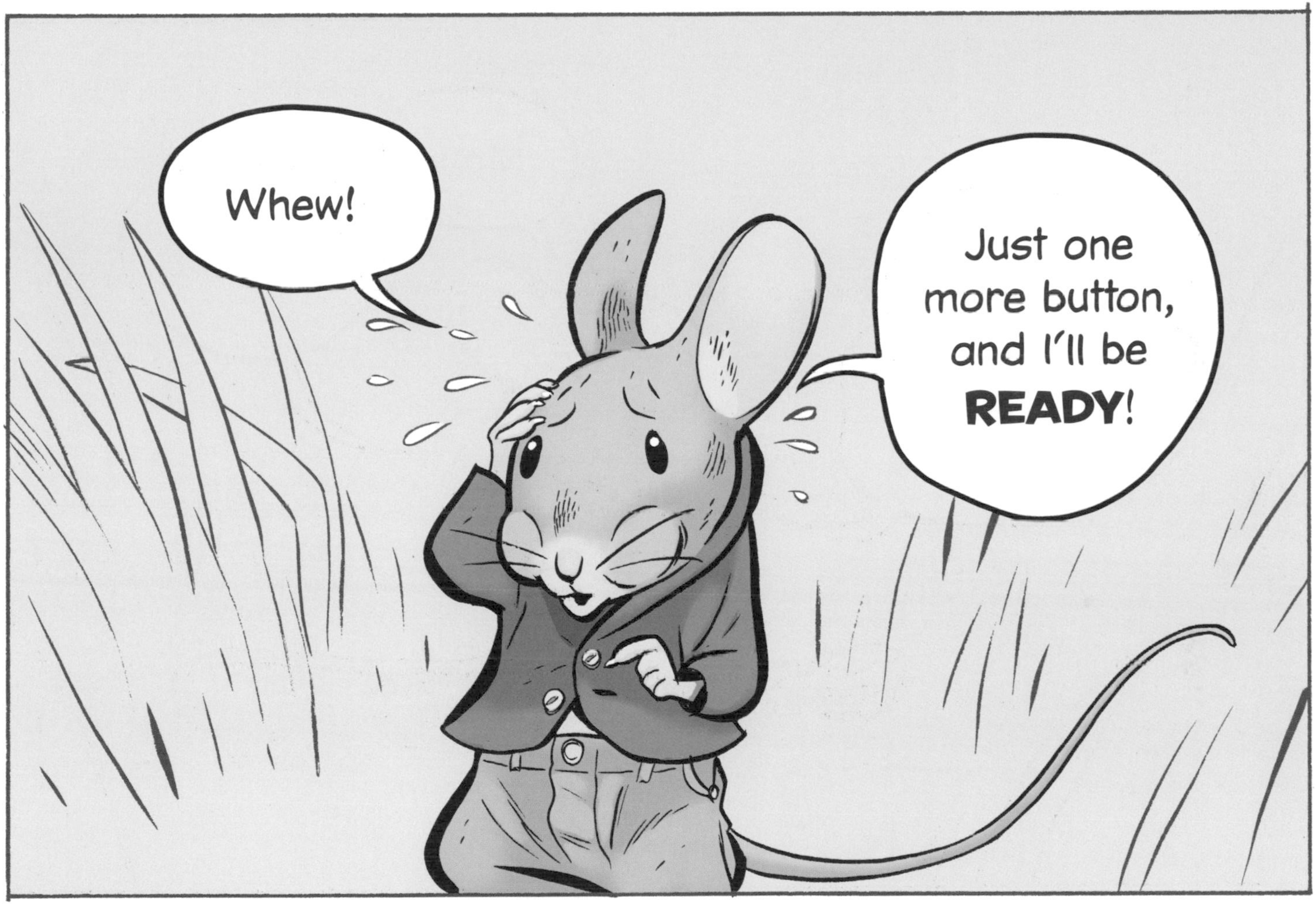
Whew!
Just one more button, and I'll be **READY**!

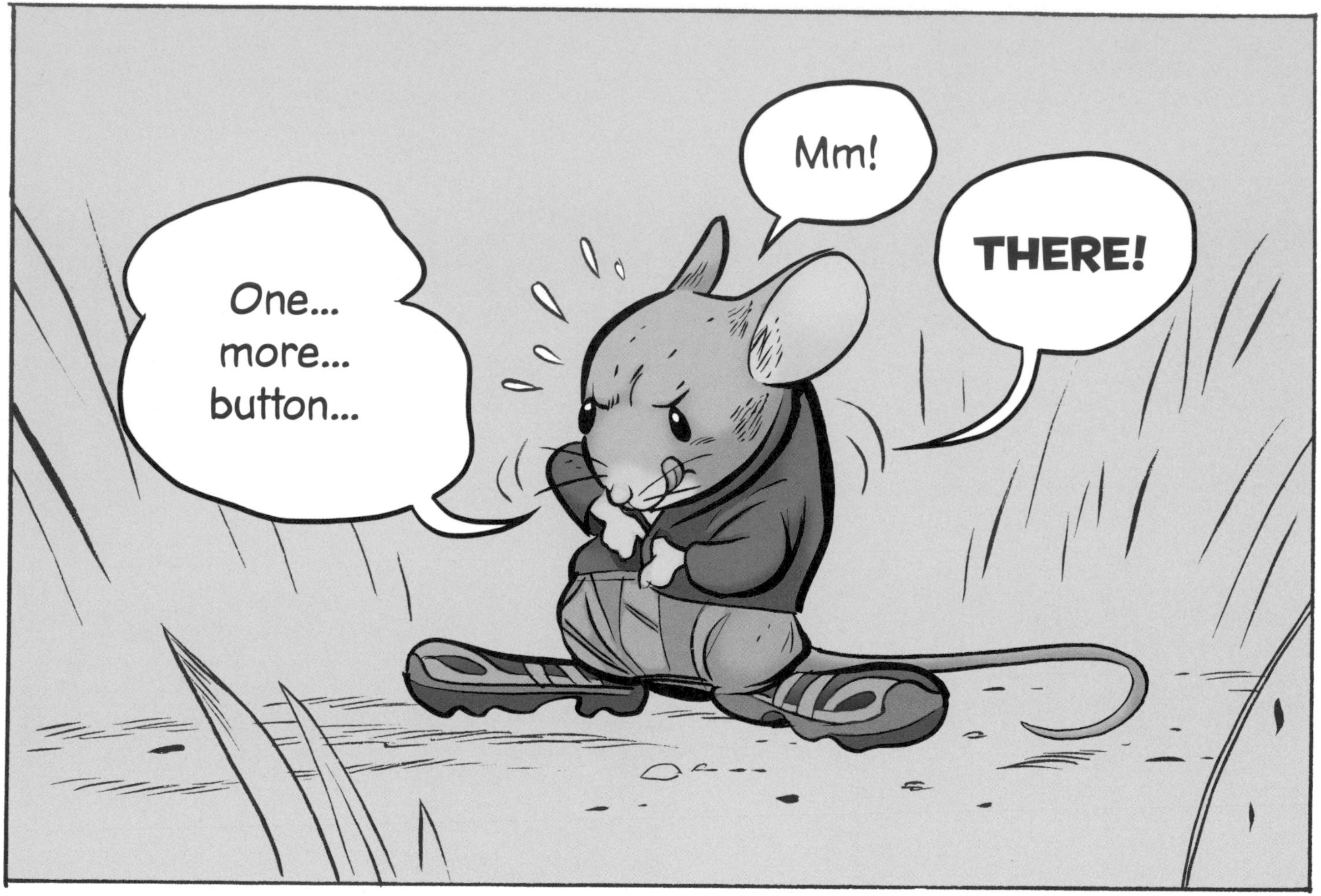
One... more... button...
Mm!
THERE!

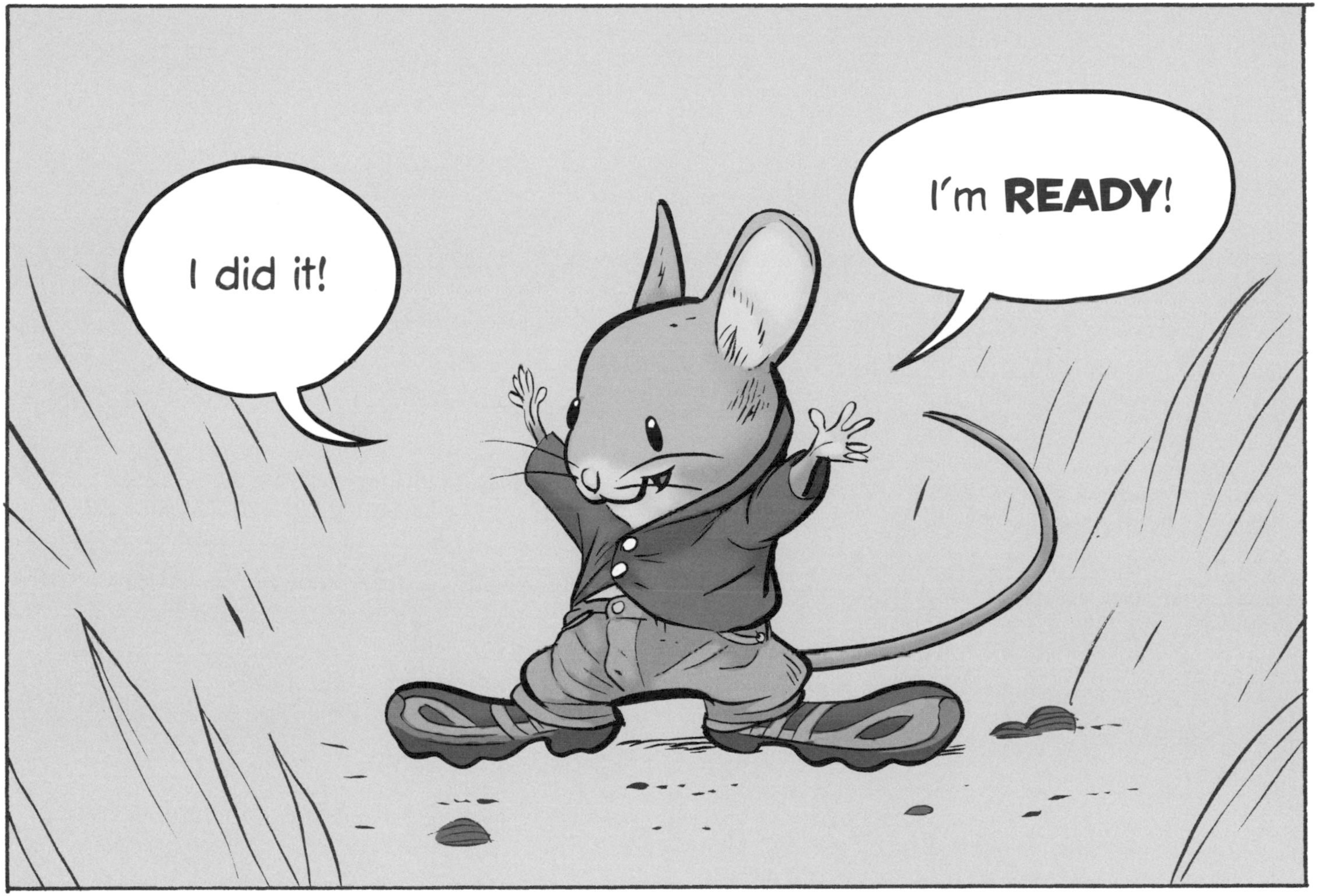
I did it!
I'm **READY**!

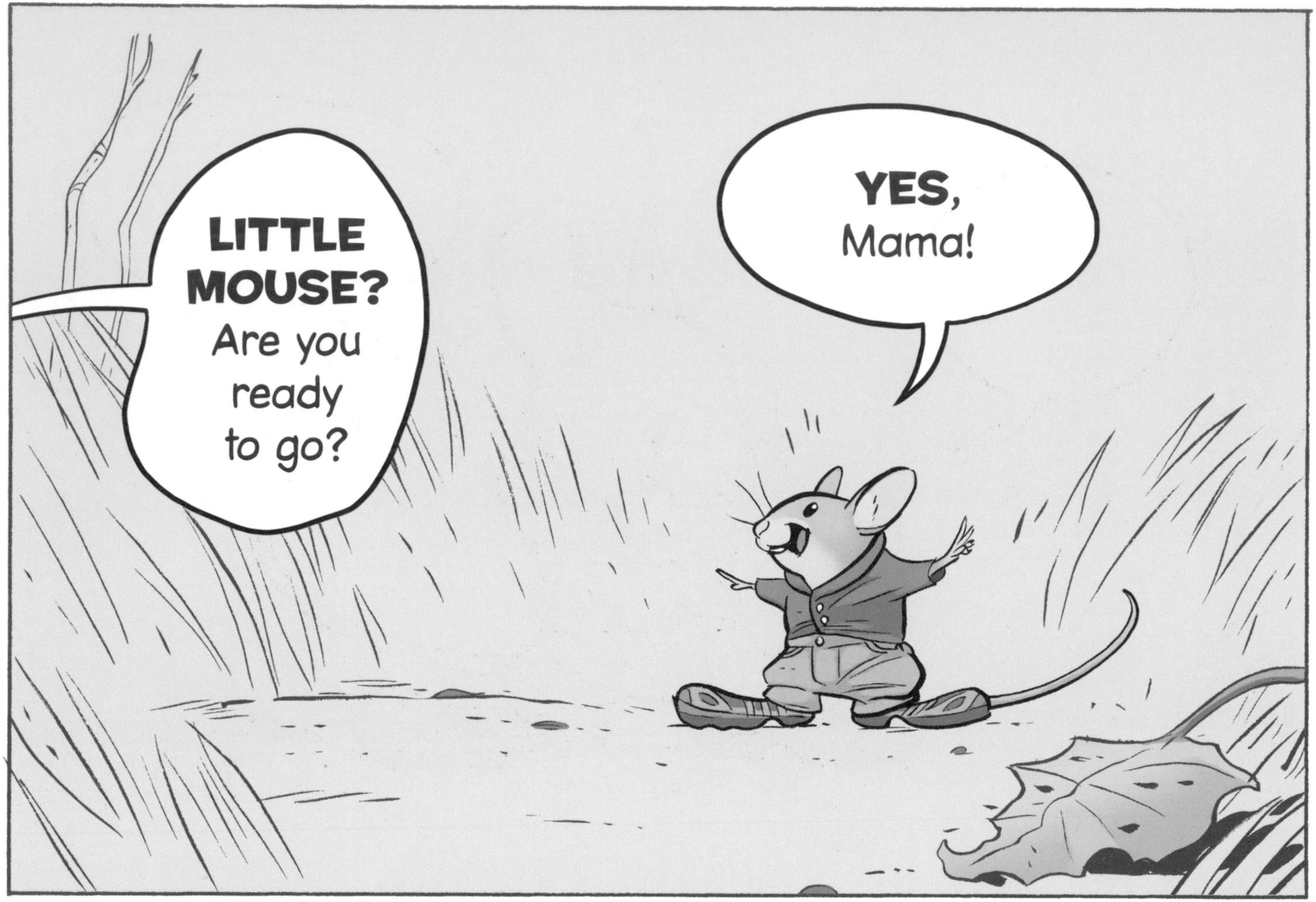
LITTLE MOUSE? Are you ready to go?
YES, Mama!

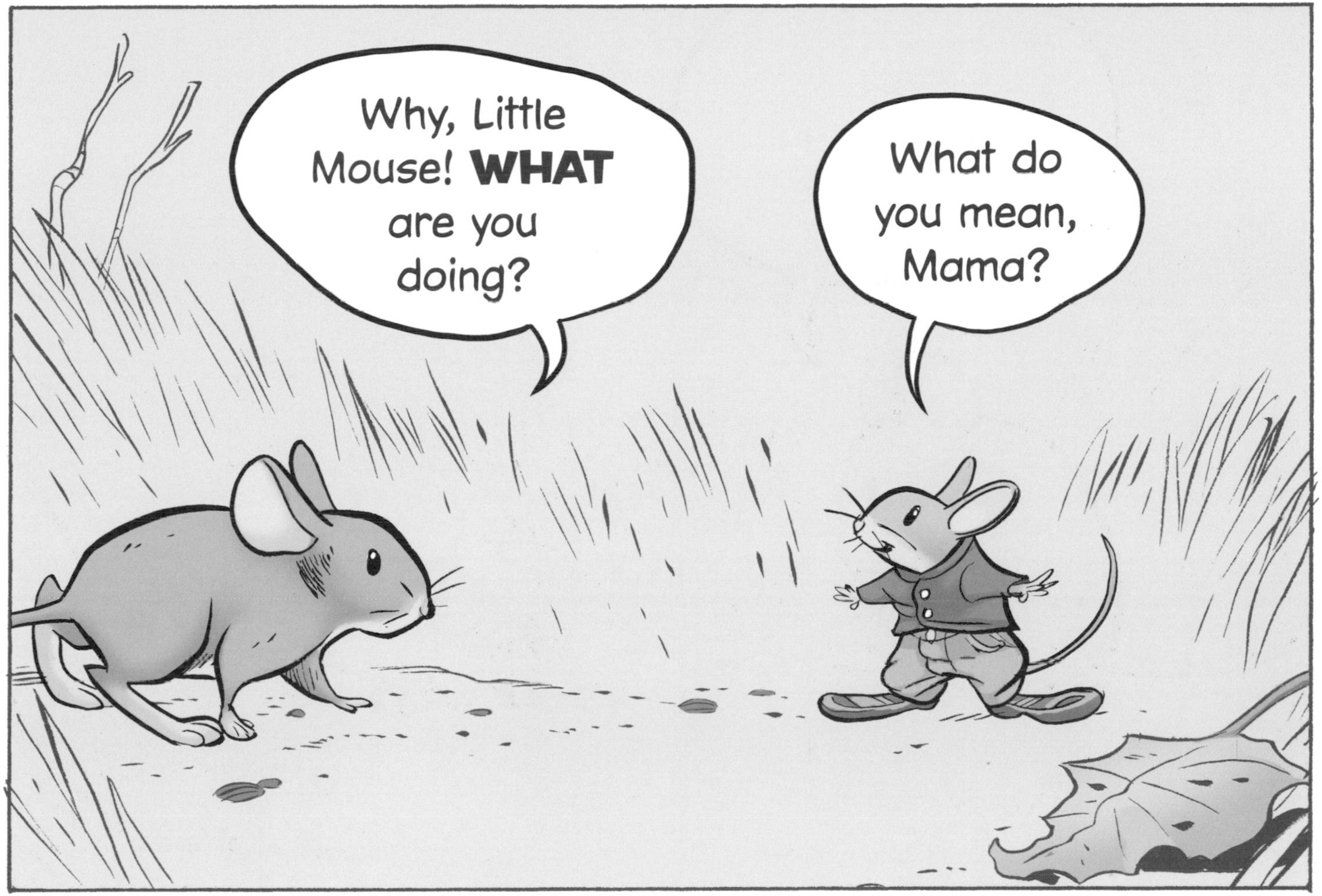
Why, Little Mouse! **WHAT** are you doing?
What do you mean, Mama?

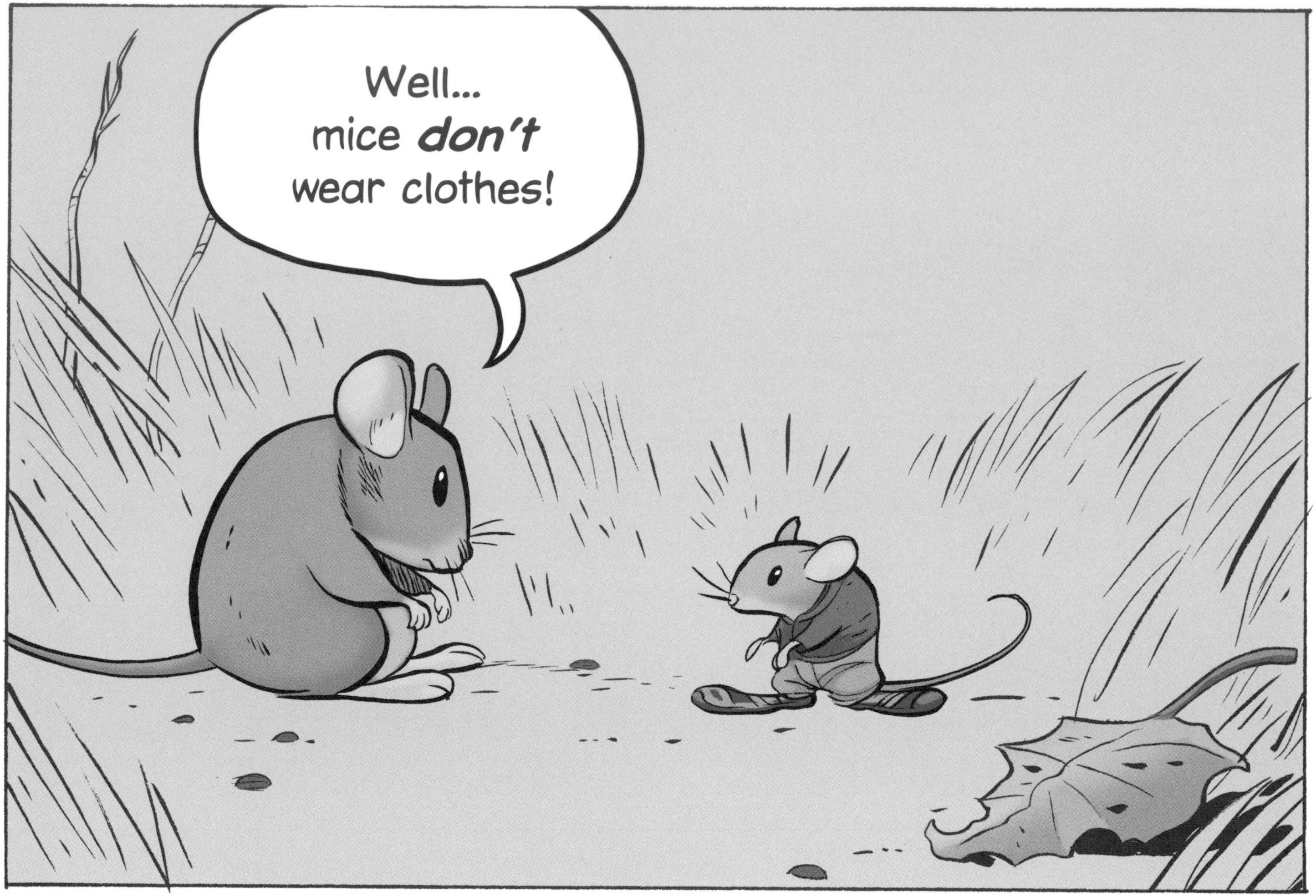
Well... mice *don't* wear clothes!

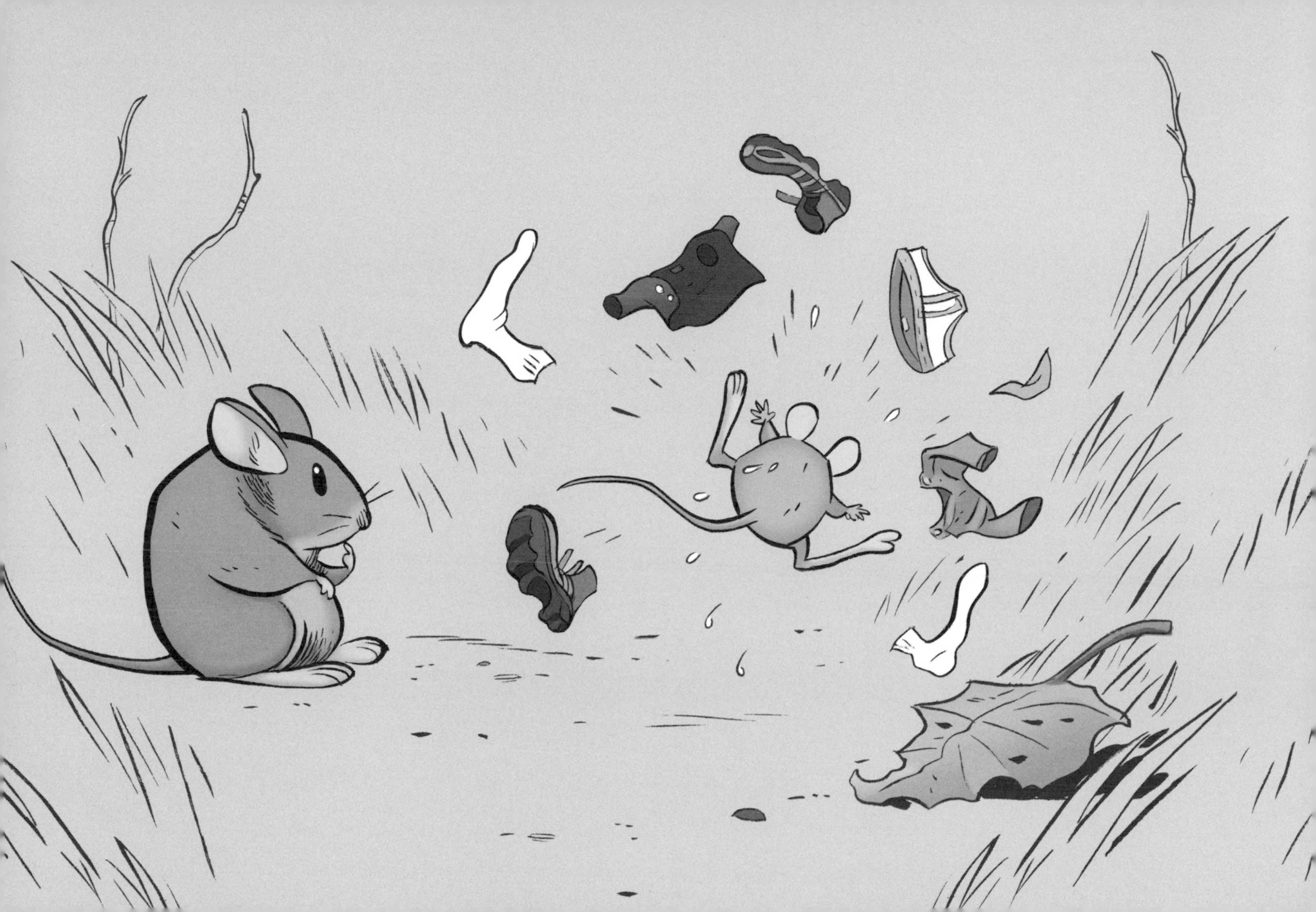

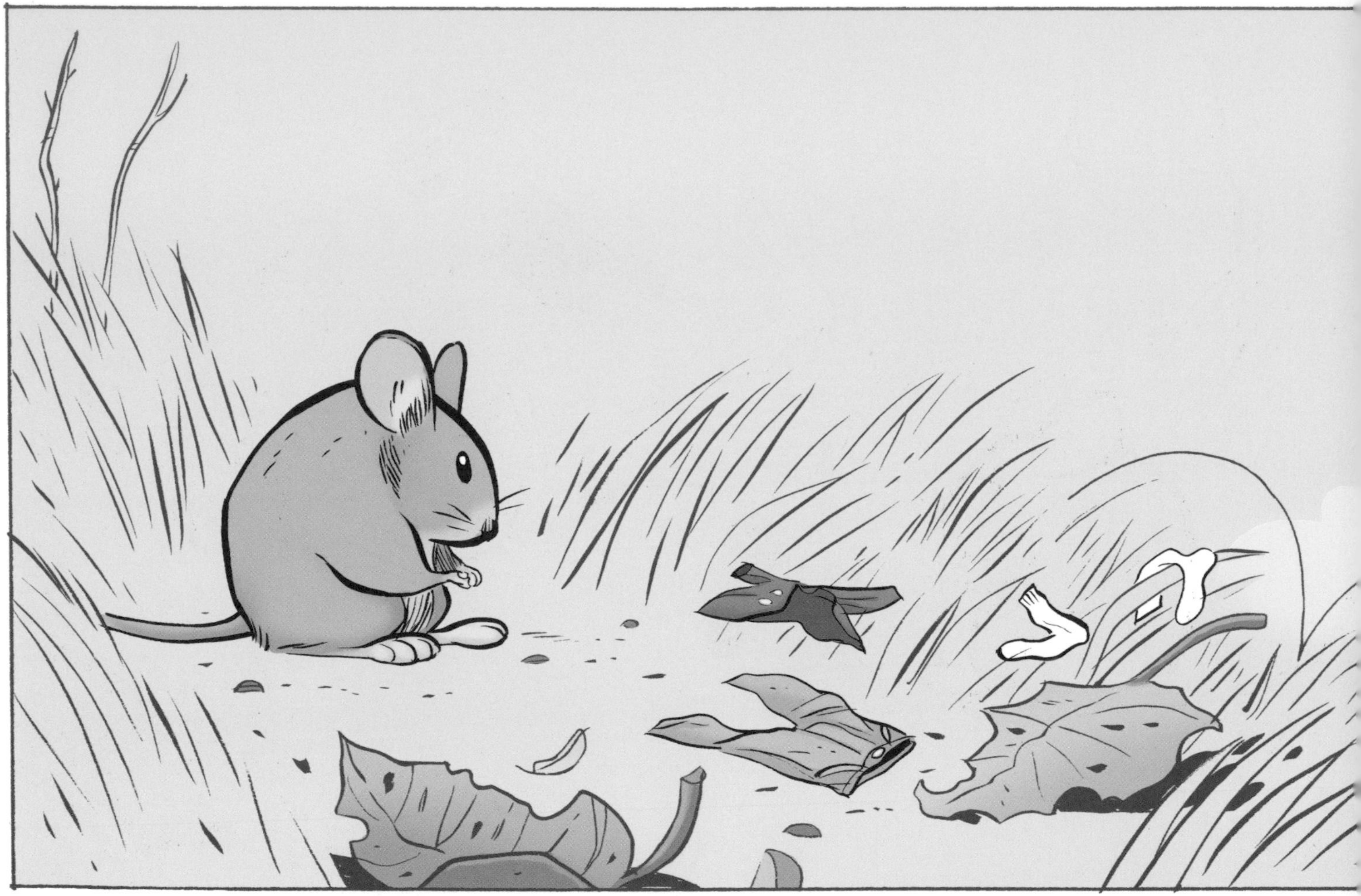

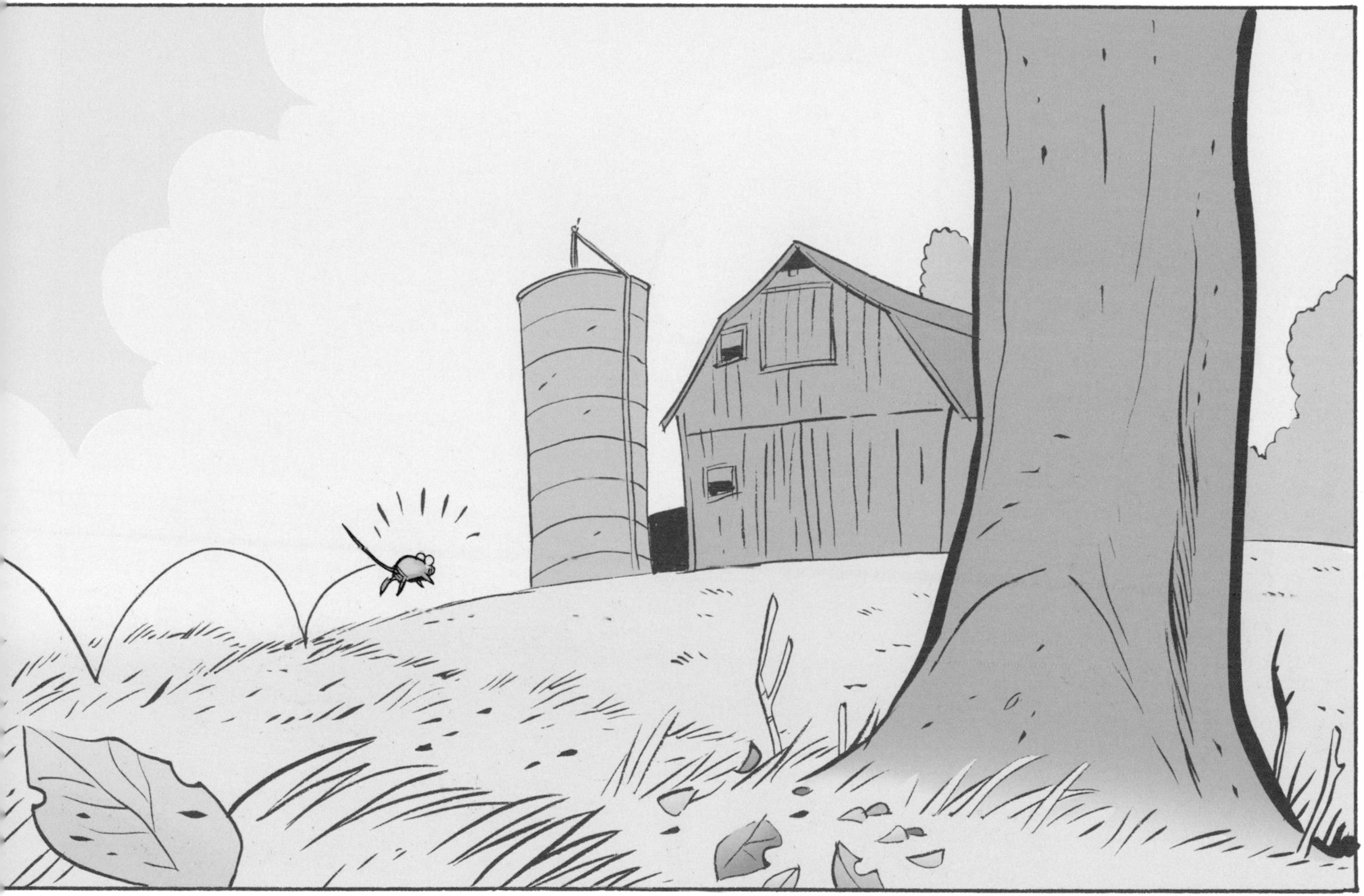

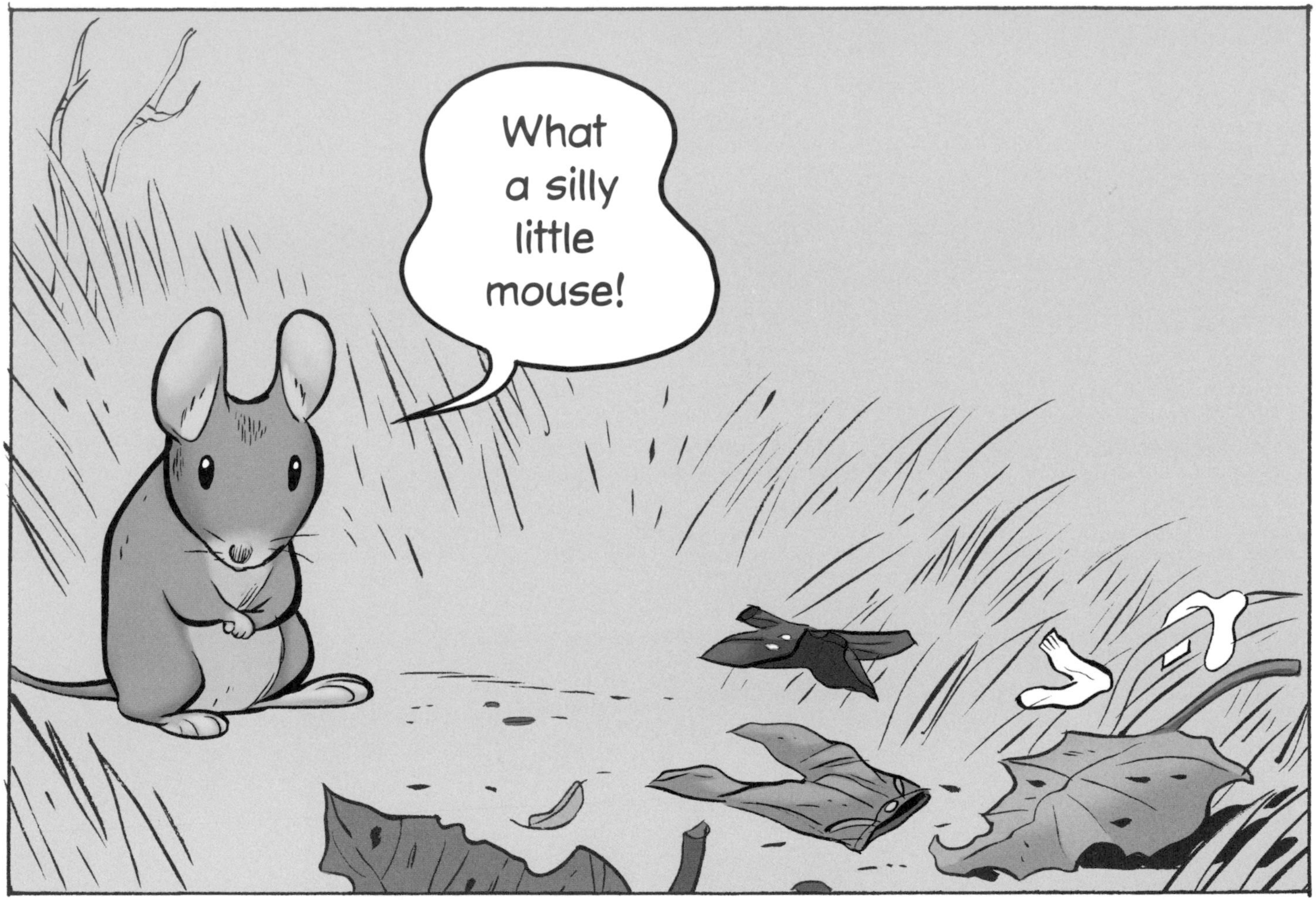
What a silly little mouse!

THE END

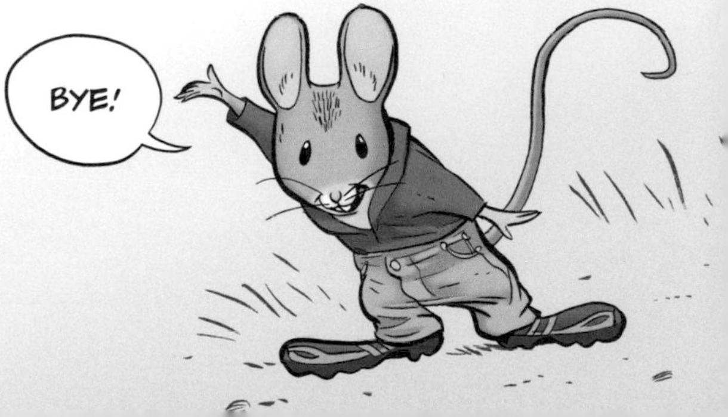
BYE!

ABOUT THE AUTHOR

When **JEFF SMITH** was growing up in a small town in Ohio, he loved cartooning, but he never imagined all the places comics would take him. With the help of his wife, Vijaya, Jeff created, published, and sold his comic book *BONE*. Jeff hadn't created *BONE* specifically for kids, but his fantastic tale of three cousins lost in a strange land appealed to all readers, including children, and it went on to sell millions of copies. *BONE* won multiple Eisner and Harvey Awards, and *TIME* called it one of the ten greatest graphic novels of all time. In 2008, Jeff's work was the subject of a major museum exhibit at the Wexner Center Galleries in Columbus, Ohio. His other books include *Shazam! The Monster Society of Evil* and *RASL*. This is his first book created just for young readers.

HOW TO "TOON INTO READING"

in a few simple steps:

Our goal is to get kids reading—and we know kids LOVE comics. We publish award-winning early readers in comics form for elementary and early middle school, and present them in three levels.

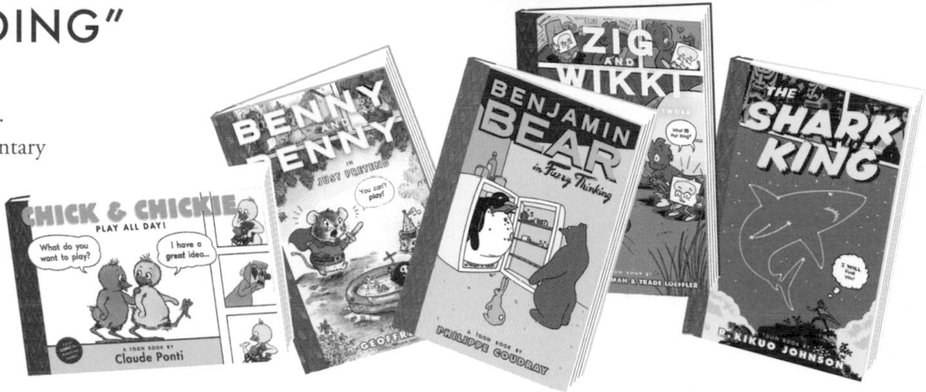
CHICK & CHICKIE
PLAY ALL DAY!
What do you want to play?
I have a great idea...
Claude Ponti
BENNY AND PENNY
JUST PRETEND
You can't play!
BENJAMIN BEAR
in Fuzzy Thinking
PHILIPPE COUDRAY
ZIG AND WIKKI
THE SHARK KING
R. KIKUO JOHNSON

1 FIND THE RIGHT BOOK

Veteran teacher Cindy Rosado tells what makes a good book for beginning and struggling readers alike: "A vetted vocabulary, plenty of picture clues, repetition, and a clear and compelling story. Also, the book shouldn't be too easy—or the reader won't learn, but neither should it be too hard—or he or she may get discouraged."

The **TOON INTO READING!**™ program is designed for beginning readers and works wonders with reluctant readers.

2 GUIDE YOUNG READERS

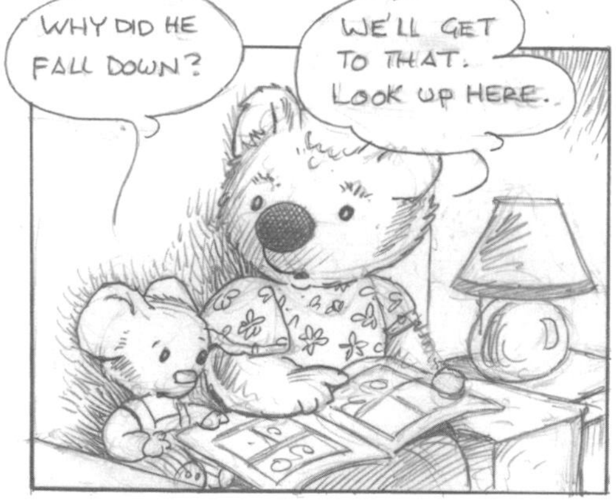
WHY DID HE FALL DOWN?
WE'LL GET TO THAT. LOOK UP HERE.

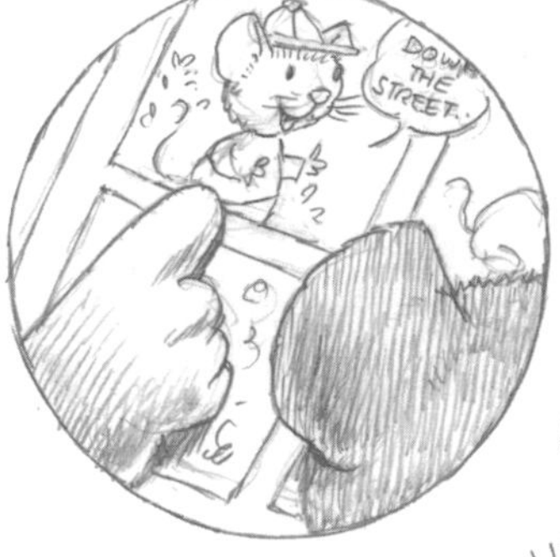
DOWN THE STREET.

What works?

Keep your fingertip below the character that is speaking.

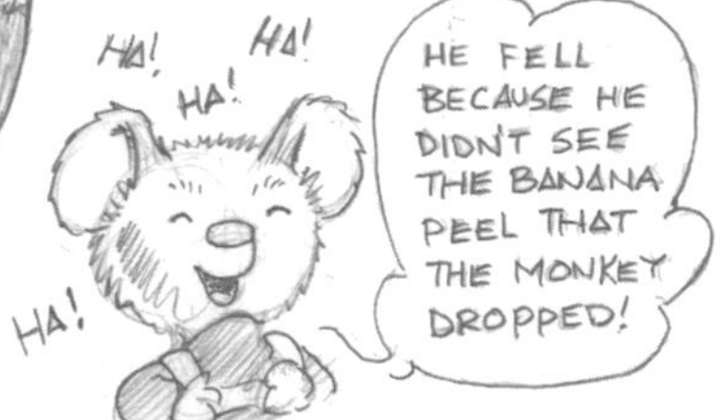
HA! HA! HA! HA!
HE FELL BECAUSE HE DIDN'T SEE THE BANANA PEEL THAT THE MONKEY DROPPED!

3 LET THEM GUESS

Comics provide a large amount of context for the words, so let young readers make informed guesses, and don't over-correct. In this panel, the artist shows a pirate ship, two pirate hats, and two pirate flags the first time the word "PIRATE" is introduced.

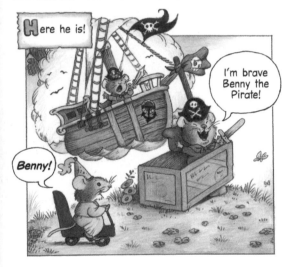

Here he is!
I'm brave Benny the Pirate!
Benny!

4 GET OUT THE CRAYONS

Kids see the hand of the author in a comic and it makes them want to tell their own stories. Encourage them to talk, write and draw!

5 TAKE TIME WITH SILENT PANELS

Comics use panels to mark time, and silent panels count. Look and "read" even when there are no words. Often, humor is all in the timing!

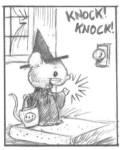

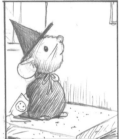

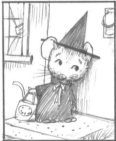

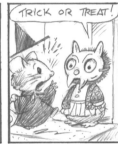

KNOCK! KNOCK!
TRICK OR TREAT!

6 HAVE FUN WITH BALLOONS

Comics use various kinds of balloons.

MOMMY?
BALLOON TAIL POINTS TO MOUTH
Ooow! LOOK! MOMMY'S SHOES!
BUBBLES POINT TO HEAD
Oops!
JAGGED BALLOONS DENOTE EXCLAMATIONS
PLUNK!

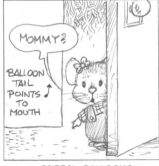

SPEECH BALLOONS

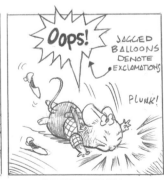

THOUGHT BALLOONS

SOUND EFFECTS